Once

A Collection of Short Stories by Jersey Writers

Published by

Jersey Writers Limited

1st edition 2015

Copyright ©Jersey Writers Limited.

ISBN 978-1508734680

Cover design by Lauren Radley

www.laurenradley.com

Edited by Julia Hunt and Jon Stasiak

www.jerseywriters.org

This book is dedicated to Jersey's heritage.

Thank you for buying this collection of stories. We hope you enjoy your literary tour of Jersey.

25% of profits raised from sales will be going to help Jersey Heritage preserve our island's most important sites.

The remainder will be used to support Jersey Writers Limited in its services to writers in Jersey.

Introduction

Once upon a time there was an island...

From castles to cottages, museums to menhirs, Jersey's heritage encompasses a wide range of sites. Some are beautiful, some are fascinating, some are heartbreaking, but each has a story to tell.

Over 20 Jersey writers decided to group together in the first year of the Channel Islands Heritage Festival to publish this anthology. We selected the sites that inspired us the most, invented characters who could have lived in Jersey at different points in history, and created a fictional celebration of our island's rich heritage.

The stories you read here will take you on a voyage around our island. They will take you through time and through heritage, through landscapes of the past and landscapes of the present. If your imagination is ready, let us begin.

A Tour of Jersey's Heritage

Our collection of stories starts in the centre of the island at Hamptonne Country Life Museum, with a post-war coming of age tale. *First Love* gives you a glimpse of Jersey's agricultural heritage through the eyes of a young boy, falling in love for the first time.

We then head north-west to the least developed part of the island and the exposed headland of Grosnez. The ruins of the 14th century castle are the setting for *On the Edge*, a story about a relationship going wrong.

The steep cliffs of Plemont are the backdrop for *The Last Falcon*, a moving tale about German soldiers and local wildlife during the Second World War.

Passing through northern parishes, which could have witnessed Occupation stories like *Liberating Jamie*, we head south.

St Helier is the setting for *V for Victory* and *A Forbidden Kiss*, stories that place us firmly in the Occupation and the struggles Islanders endured during the Second World War. *Ouelle Est Gaûchie* reflects upon this era through the eyes of the Jersey women who sewed the Occupation Tapestry.

The memories recalled in *Remember* focus on Jersey Museum and the restored Merchant's House at 9 Pier Road.

May 1661, Jersey looks at the island post-reformation, when a loyal wife has troubling suspicions about her husband.

The town shares its name with a hermit who lived on Jersey's south coast, near the site of Elizabeth Castle, in the sixth century. *Helerius Unmasked* gently mocks the island's first saint, while neatly introducing us to the Vikings who came to raid the Channel Islands towards the end of the first Millennium.

Threat of invasion from France intensified between the 1770s and the 1830s, when many 'Conway' towers and 'Martello'-like towers were built around the coast. On the east side of the island, Archirondel Tower is the location for the ironically-titled *Liberation,* a story about a woman freeing herself from an abusive husband. The tower itself is now run by Jersey Heritage as basic accommodation. Many others, such as the one in *A Knock at the Door*, a story about preconceptions, have been incorporated into private houses.

Mont Orgueil Castle, above the village of Gorey, dates back to the 13th century when Jersey pledged allegiance to England, then at war with France. The castle has inspired stories across the eras: *P'tun 1625* is a courtroom drama centred on the witch trials of the 17th century; *The Wedding Gift* is a contemporary story with flashbacks to the Occupation; *Ghostly Encounters* is a spritely comedy; and *When the Tide Turns* is about how it's never too late to start again.

La Hougue Bie is one of the oldest heritage sites in Jersey. Its Neolithic burial chamber dates back to 3,000 BC. The medieval church on top of the site features in *Miracles Will Happen*.

Travelling west, we pass over bays and headlands to St Brelade. La Cotte is the setting for *Mammoth*, a story about Palaeolithic hunters who inhabited the area about 250,000 years ago. It is also the scene for *Sea Bride*, a mysterious tale of the perils of falling in love with a mermaid.

Our literary tour continues along the Atlantic coast, where, amongst the sand dunes, you will find Bronze Age sites such as the Broken Menhir, the Little Menhir and The Ossuary, the inspiration for *Her Daughter at the Dolmens*.

We conclude our collection and our journey at the Barge Aground, a 1930s folly above Jersey's longest beach, where *Warm Sand* tells a story of the restorative powers of a beautiful landscape.

Table of Contents

FIRST LOVE

GWYN GARFIELD-BENNETT

Gwyn is a professional journalist, broadcaster and writer. She has been a newsreader for national television with ITN and the BBC as well as writing for national newspapers and magazines. She now works in PR/Social media marketing, but writes spec TV drama scripts in her spare time and is due to publish her first novel in 2015.

First Love – By Gwyn Garfield-Bennett

He walks towards his destiny, heart beating fast, hands gripping the small bunch of hedgerow flowers so tightly he might crush them. He's oblivious to the golden coated Jersey cows who look up from their grazing with dark heavily lashed eyes. He's oblivious to the bright sun and blue sky, the fields of emerald jewels laden with summer salad crops, and he doesn't smell the scents of summer on the breeze: fresh cut grass, dust, the sickly perfume of hogweed heads which line the road.

He is nearly there. He passes by the row of farm workers' cottages every day on his way to and from school, each time holding his breath and praying for a glimpse of her. Today he is going to knock on her door. She will open it with a huge smile and he will offer up his flowers, and maybe, just maybe she will give him a thank you kiss before saying goodbye. Then he will breathe again.

Matthew slows down as he nears her door, hands clammy with sweat that isn't from the heat. He can't feel his legs as they automatically take each step closer. He also doesn't see the granite rock which protrudes from the road where years of rain and use have worn away its covering. His foot finds it. Suddenly his mouth is full of dust and the pinks and purples of his love are strewn across the road.

For a moment he is stunned, winded and then he registers the sound of a door opening, footsteps and he can smell her, freshly washed: roses, springtime and love all in one breath.

"Are you all right?" She helps him from the ground, picking up his school bag, gently dusting him down. Her loose blond hair brushes against his face and he can't help notice the swell of her breasts as she leans into him, the softness of her pale skin - so unlike the other farm workers.

His face is burning and he glances at the ruined flowers.

"Oh were those for your mother? I'll help you pick some more if you like?" He shakes his head, he needs to be gone. She reaches towards him and takes a leaf from his hair.

"You'll be just fine, it's Matthew isn't it?" He nods and as she hands him his books their fingers touch momentarily and a tingle runs through his body. He is off.

A few seconds later he turns to see her going back inside,

"Thank you Annie."

Matthew runs through the yard at Hamptonne, past the stables and apple crushing barn, past the main house and pigsties to his home and the safety of its granite walls. Every building is built from the solid stone of the island's core and even today's relentless sun can't penetrate it. He loves the granite of Hamptonne, it isn't a soulless dull grey as you'd imagine, it almost seems to have a life of its own. Shimmering shards of quartz captured within it, each block an individual with its own shape and contour, one with flashes of rust and

15

pink, another almost black. All around him the houses and barns rise up solidly from the ground, reassuring.

The kitchen is empty. It's his favourite room soaked in the aroma of generations of cooking. In the winter he'll go and sit in the wooden armchair by the fire, but now in the height of summer he strips off his shoes and socks and stands on the floor with bare feet, letting the stone flags draw the heat from them. He's been known to lie on it after a particularly hot walk home from school, staring up at the wooden ceiling or at the sepia photograph on the wall of his grandparents in traditional Jersey dress. His grandfather proudly holding the tether of a Jersey cow and his grandmother beside him in the customary white cloth bonnet and apron. She is holding a wood and metal bucket which Matthew always imagines to be full of milk. Today he feels too vulnerable to lie prostrate, he'd rather hide in a corner like a dog licking his wounds, hopes dashed. The anger at himself wells up inside threatening to turn to tears.

Matthew hears his mother's footsteps and struggles to regain his composure, her sympathy might tip him over and he's 11 now, he shouldn't be crying. He's lucky she's preoccupied with housework and doesn't notice the falseness of his smile.

"Good day at school?" She carries some bread loaves she's just collected from the bake house and busies herself storing them in the pantry.

"Yes thank you," is all he can muster.

"Grandpa has a surprise for you in the back garden." His mother doesn't have time to say another word; he rushes outside, sore knees and wounded pride forgotten.

Outside, his grandfather is putting the finishing touches to a small run which contains a young cockerel.

"There you are lad, come here."

"A cockerel, Grandpa?"

"He's yours. I want you to take good care of him and show me you can fatten him up good and proper for us. Then if you do, well, I'll give you a couple of hens to take care of."

"All my own, Grandpa?"

"All your own." The old man smiles at the young boy, remembering his own excitement at his first responsibility, too many years ago to want to count.

The next day Matthew almost jogs all the way from school, eager to be home. When he reaches Annie's cottage he slows, looking for her. He spots her in an upstairs window and she waves. He shyly half lifts his hand in return. Then he is off home, not to the cool kitchen, but straight into the garden where the cockerel is scratching in the earth.

"Percy, I've saved you some treats," he whispers to the bird. From his bag he pulls out a half-eaten apple, some crusts and some raisins. "I've just seen Annie, she waved." Nervously the cockerel approaches the food the boy holds, snatching and eating it. Matthew sits watching, chatting to him about his day.

The air that night is heavy and sticky with heat, like someone has mixed cornflour in the atmosphere. At bedtime Matthew hangs out of his open bedroom window and whispers down into the garden, "Good night Percy." He looks out over

17

Hamptonne's roof tops to the distant row of cottages where a faint glow shows Annie is home. He imagines her getting ready for sleep; she'll be up at 5am with the sunrise for work. Tonight he'll sleep well, dreaming of Annie and Percy and what could be.

The earthy smell of autumn is in the air and the first signs of smoke from chimneys heralds the summer's passing and the chill of its ghostly remains. Matthew kicks at piles of leaves as he walks, stopping at hedgerows to pick blackberries which he collects in his empty lunch pot with an eat one, save one rhythm.

Past Annie's cottage and she's there at her window. She waves and he smiles and waves back, taking in the picture of her beauty, memorising it for later retrieval.

At home Percy has grown into a fine cockerel, strutting around his run, master of his domain, no longer the shy little bird Matthew had first been given.

"Percy, Percy, chuck chuck," Matthew calls to him and is rewarded by the cockerel running straight to his voice. The boy opens the run and Percy hops onto his lap, taking the blackberries offered to him. Matthew sits there stroking him, his small hands running over the shimmering purple, black and white of the bird's feathers. He's so soft, so perfect. Boy and bird sit nestled together for warmth until Percy spots a worm attempting to bury for safety and jumps from Matthew to feed some more.

The fields have turned from green to brown and the canopy of trees, which sheltered Matthew from the sun on his summer walks home, are skeletal branches. He's wrapped up against the winter chill, nose pink, eyes watering from the winds blown across the seas from colder climes.

Matthew walks past Annie's cottage but there's no sign of her, its empty eyes look back at him reflecting the dark grey skies. At home the kitchen is warm and welcoming, a fire in the grate and a pot hanging above. Matthew drops his school bag, takes some scraps from the food cupboard and goes into the garden.

"Percy, Percy... chuck chuck..." The run is empty.

He checks the small chicken house. Empty. "Percy, Percy..." He calls to him. Searching in the bushes, his stomach knotting with anxiety. No sign.

Into the house.

"Mum, Mum... it's Percy, I can't find him." His mother comes into the kitchen, there's a reassuring but sympathetic look on her face. She moves towards him but he backs away, alarm bells clanging in his head.

"Sweetheart, Grandpa came for him earlier. Said you'd done a great job with the bird."

"Came for him?" Matthew's voice struggles to escape his throat.

"Yes he's taken him to Annie in the end barn."

"No."

"You knew this was going to happen, why Grandpa gave him to you... Matthew, Matthew..." but he is gone, the door wide open and scattered crusts on the floor.

He runs as fast as he has ever run in his whole life. He knows what happens in the end barn. The barn where the doors stay shut to keep out flies and keep in the stench of death.

He slips on the damp stone nearly colliding with some cider barrels, grazing his hand. He doesn't feel anything, sheer panic has taken over his body, he mustn't be too late.

As Matthew approaches the end barn he sees his grandfather's back in the doorway. He's talking to someone, it's going to be fine, he has just arrived.

"Grandpa, Grandpa..." he calls out. His grandfather turns and smiles, oblivious to the urgency.

"Matthew, lad. You did a great job with that bird." He smiles again and opens the door for Matthew to see. At first his eyes don't register the form in the doorway, but as he gets closer he sees it's Annie. Not the after-school Annie he knows, this Annie has hair tied back and her work clothes are bloodied. Caught on the fibres of the fabric are tiny soft downy white feathers struggling to escape.

Then he sees what she is holding. A plucked chicken, its naked body headless and legless, ready for the pot. Behind her is a wooden stool surrounded by piles of feathers which catch the wind and stir, shimmering purple and black in the pale winter light.

"Annie's done a beautiful job of him hasn't she? He's a fine bird, Matthew. Good job lad, good job. Your mother will make us all a nice dinner tonight."

Behind his grandpa Annie smiles at Matthew. He looks from one to the other. They're both smiling at him, expecting, waiting. Tears well in his eyes and he runs from them.

Spring is forcing itself from the ground. Shoots of green mix with yellow daffodils and the sky is filled with the return of bird song not heard since last summer. The granite walls that run along the road have sat barren through the winter, but are once again being dressed with colour and life. Matthew walks home from school lost in concentration as he kicks a small rock down the road. He doesn't notice the reprise of life around him.

He approaches Annie's cottage and she's there in the window. Annie raises her hand to wave, a smile on her face, but Matthew doesn't even look in her direction. Her hand falls to her side as she watches his back disappear along the road.

THE LAST FALCON

ROGER BAILEY

Roger has been resident in Jersey since 1979 and is passionate about the beautiful environment in which he lives. He is inspired by the scenery, the wildlife in all its forms, and by the strangest creatures of all; people.

The Last Falcon – By Roger Bailey

The pigeon was dead before it hit the water. It had not even seen the falcon and the strike was violent enough to kill it instantly. The impact was hard and brutal, but it was also too late. If the falcon had tried to hold on to the quarry they would have both ended up in the sea. Reluctantly she dropped the dead pigeon which, when it hit the water, was immediately set upon by hungry, opportunistic seagulls. The falcon pulled out of the stoop and levelled off her flight.

"It's coming this way now, Hans, and it's tired! You should be able to get it. This is the closest we have ever seen it so far, make sure that the shot counts, we won't get a second chance. Think of the bounty!"

The bird roused her feathers as she flew towards the shore, still hungry and becoming increasingly weary from her exertions. She had failed in four stoops before finally grabbing the pigeon she had just dropped: the fifth failure had sapped more of her strength. Even though she could dance on the wind it still took a lot of her energy to mount another stoop; each attempt being more tiring than the last. She surveyed the Plemont cliffs for more prey. Her stoop had alarmed a lot of other birds into flight and she scanned the skies looking for one showing a weakness, an impediment. A few broken feathers, an immature, over confident demeanour, perhaps a drooping leg; all of these things could indicate vulnerability. A message attached to the leg of a pigeon would be likely to cause that leg

23

to droop and the balance of nature is a very precise balance: that which fits best will survive.

There is a symbiosis between predator and prey which dictates that whichever of the two best fits the environment for the duration of their life and death duel may survive; the other may not. The pursued can often outpace the pursuer, but sometimes the reverse is true particularly if the prey is weak or injured, or otherwise impeded. The pigeon only knew that the extra weight tied to its leg made it that bit more difficult to fly at top speed, as it would need to if it were to outrun a peregrine falcon. Equally, the hunter did not know what caused the slight drag displayed by the pigeon in flight, and all it knew of the tightly bound package, that was the message, was that it was inedible.

For now she was content to observe, it would be some time yet before she could confidently start to gain the height needed to identify and drop on another disadvantaged bird. It would be good if she could pick out a possible target before she began her rise. Anything that helped her to be more efficient, to use less energy, was to her advantage. Most of her stoops ended in failure, but she needed to eat every day so giving up was not an option for so long as the day stayed light.

Early morning light had given the cliffs a pale yellow hue. Later in the day they turned to orange and then almost red before changing to a bluer spectrum as the evening closed in. Blue sky reflected in blue sea and the waves broke over the smooth sand, dry now, as the tide rose. Rock pools awaited their regular water change and the life clinging to the rocks held tight in anticipation of their twice daily immersion. The ebbing and flowing of the tide meant nothing to the falcon, she had no idea how great was its influence on her prey. Instinct and experience has taught her everything but she cared not for the past, nor did she invest her efforts in the future. She knew that nothing had ever happened in the past and that nothing ever would happen in the future. Everything that happens, happens only in the present and that is where her attention lay.

Concrete block bunkers and gun mountings with their heavy grey metal and squared off permanence were incongruous with the rugged cliffs and fields of bracken which changed so dramatically with the seasons. A concrete tower stood over the headland giving the watchful soldiers the same advantages the falcon had when she alighted on her craggy outcrops. One well designed and strategically placed bunker could be a great asset in the protection of a large area of coastal cliffs. Construction was a challenge but then there was no shortage of manpower, and the German intention was a permanent stay. Aesthetics were not a consideration for the architects of these observatories and defences. Functionality was all that mattered so concrete, buttressed as necessary, was the raw material. The fact that the scenic views from some of these observation points could only be described as stunning was entirely coincidental.

"I didn't come here to shoot bloody birds, I'm a soldier, I should be pointing my gun at the enemy not at some defenceless bunch of feathers." Hans said.

"You know why we have to do this, these falcons are killing the carrier pigeons flying to and from the Fatherland, the messages they carry could make a difference to the entire war, they might even help us to get home quicker." This was Jurgen, the older of the two soldiers manning the observation tower.

"War doesn't have to be like this, Jurgen, destroying birds, wreaking landscapes, crushing whole societies, is there supposed to be some point to all this? Dear Adolf told us we would sweep across Europe taking everything in our stride and be home again by Christmas. Sure, the French and the Belgians gave up without much of a fight but the British are not going to roll over and give in any time soon, and now that the Americans are joining in we can expect a good hammering. I don't know about you but I am finding it hard to remember why I ever thought this war was a good idea. Just look at this beautiful island, tiny in the great European scheme of things, but see what we have done to it. The people are compliant because we shoot them if they are not, there are always shortages of food and fuel, these godawful concrete bunkers keep appearing in the landscape, and I am surprised that any of us survived last winter with all the shortages. The only thing we're not short of is shortages! And now we are blasting these beautiful birds from the sky."

"You should be careful where you say things like that, Hans. There are people here who would shop you to the Gestapo for even thinking those thoughts. You are right that war is a terrible thing but it is the way the world goes. You and I are here, Hans because we are too old and decrepit for the battlefront. You should be grateful to have this cushy posting instead of freezing half to death in some godforsaken trench a thousand miles from Germany."

The falcon needed to rest but there was no need for her to land. Turning her face to the wind she broadened her wings by spreading out her primary feathers to give her wings a greater surface area. The secondary feathers found their own places alongside and amongst the primaries. It was almost effortless so rather than immediately climbing on the freshening breeze she spent some moments traversing the updraft along the cliff face. Passing the place she had used as a nest just a few months earlier she paused and felt alone. Her mate and the four chicks they had raised together that spring had all gone, she knew not where. Food had been plentiful, the pigeons, which comprised most of their diet, had been very successful in raising their squabs this year and bringing up all four of her young had not been too challenging for her and her mate. They had fed the whole family without too much effort; it was not like that every year.

"I envy them their ability to fly." It was Hans again. "If I could I would fly away somewhere sunny and peaceful, somewhere with palm trees and oranges growing by the side of the road."

"Dreaming is good," replied Jurgen, "anything that can take away the boredom and drudgery of this existence has to be good."

"I dream mainly of home, Jurgen, of family and friends and music and dancing. One day maybe all of this madness will be over and the world will return to some sort of normality."

"This is normality for now my friend. What has gone before becomes irrelevant and we have no idea really about what might happen tomorrow. We have to try and enjoy the day as much as we can."

27

"Enjoy? A lot of things will have to change before I can enjoy myself." Hans was showing his relative immaturity, believing that all would be well if things just went his way a bit more. "I wish I was like that bird, floating free without a care in the world, free to roam the skies and please itself. Free to go anywhere it chooses, that is freedom, that is what I want."

It was time to think of mounting the wind to ride upwards to her next stoop, hopefully this one would be successful. The light was starting to fade; there would not be many more chances today. She noticed that there were fewer birds in flight now, many of her potential quarry were starting to settle down or head for their night time shelters. She too would have to make this decision soon, where to roost, which way was the wind blowing, where was there good shelter from the elements. She knew of many places she could use, she did not face any competition from other birds. She would simply need to assess the conditions and choose her shelter. Hunger drove her on but she did not want to hurry. She soared across the cliff face again, doing what she was best at - flying.

Of course no one knew that all the other falcons had already been killed, no one was counting. Nor did the falcon know why she had not seen any of her kind for a long time. The fact was that the occupying forces had offered a bounty on the falcons and many had taken up the challenge. The bounty was extra rations of food and fuel and everyone wanted those, soldiers and civilians alike. This was the last peregrine falcon in Jersey and now she came closer to her hunters than she had ever been, oblivious to the danger they posed. In spite of his reluctance and his admiration for the magnificent bird the German soldier knew what his duty was and what had to be done.

War was cruel but he could not be permitted to make decisions which were clearly based on emotional rather than martial considerations. His opinions were irrelevant, his feelings superfluous. If he could stop the bird, then stop it he must. Hans shouldered his shotgun and trained the foresight on the approaching bird. She was flying slowly, tired and hungry, contemplating another rise and another stoop. She roused her feathers again in anticipation of climbing the wind currents when suddenly, and only briefly, a loud bang caught her attention. Briefly, because it was the report of the shotgun being fired at her and she was mortally wounded by the first shot. The second barrel was not fired. The two German soldiers, and the wild rugged cliffs of Plemont, watched mournfully as the last falcon fell lifeless to the ground.

ON THE EDGE

BETH DANIELS

Beth was born in South Africa and spent many years in Zimbabwe. She now lives in Jersey, where she attended Creative Writing Classes which sparked her love of writing.

On The Edge – By Beth Daniels

As the plane lifts off the runway I gaze down at the island for the last time. Below me the white sands of St Ouen's Bay stretch from Corbiére Lighthouse to L'Etacq. The plane banks away, and the island, looking like a huge patch-work counterpane, soon disappears from view. A pink glow in the east heralds another glorious day, but I won't be there to enjoy it. I can never return to Jersey.

On the rugged cliffs at the most north-westerly point of Jersey stands a ruined 14th century castle. Nothing remains except the gatehouse. For centuries Grosnez has been left to dream of past days and heroic battles. In the summer months the walks round the headland are spectacular, with azure blue seas breaking gently in puffs of white spume against the cliffs below. Then the islands of Guernsey, Sark and Herm seem close. But in the winter the gales howl and tear at the rocks and sparse grasses, almost shaking the ruins to destruction. Then the sea angrily lashes at the cliffs and the other islands are hidden in the mists.

It was on such a winter's day that James proudly brought me, his bride, to explore my new island home. Breathless with new-found happiness, I'd fallen in love with Grosnez and its wild, haunting beauty. The grey-green seas battering the shores held me spellbound and when the wind suddenly stilled as though to draw breath, I held my breath too.

31

"Darling, don't laugh, but I'm enchanted with this castle. I can feel the thrilling atmosphere all round me. What wonderful things these old stones could tell me."

James laughed and held me close against the gusting wind.

"Wait till you see Jersey in the spring, Lucy. It's more beautiful than you can imagine, then you must feel the hot sun in summer and swim in that beautiful, inviting sea!"

My innocent delight in his beloved island was infectious.

"There's so much more to explore and experience, my darling," he whispered seductively in my ear as the wind strengthened. "Especially you, and I know you will love my island."

"Not as much as I love you, darling James. Just look at the castle! Magic! It's trying to tell me something," I laughed. "It seems to be pulling at me …"

"Just like I'm pulling you away, Lucy. Come along, darling. It's mighty cold, and what say you to hot chocolate, and muffins dripping with butter...?"

I also visited the other castles in Jersey, as I had my own little car. Each one was delightful in its own way, but they didn't thrill me as much as my special castle, which I visited as often as I could. I went back to it again and again and never grew tired of its changing moods. I learned about its brave past, and while James was at work I spent hours sitting on the headland reading and dreaming, and imagining heroic battles and stories about the soldiers that guarded the fort.

I would then return to our little cottage with its old pink granite walls nestling under weather-worn tiles, and at the front door I always paused to look up at the comforting sight of the traditional granite lintel with hearts carved around the initials of some long-forgotten Jersey couple.

Then came the day when I stopped and looked at the stone initials in a different way.

"I wish our names were there," I sighed. "They'd look so permanent — forever." I was deeply saddened because James was less affectionate than usual. Perhaps he was worried about his work. When I told him about my Grosnez visits he seemed annoyed.

"It's about time you gave up this nonsense, Lucy, and looked for a job. You're wasting your time mooning about the countryside."

"But darling, you didn't want me to work. We planned to start a family."

But James just shook his head impatiently and stalked off, leaving me hurt and bewildered.

He'd changed so much. He was quieter and somehow strangely indifferent. Our happy times together exploring the beauty of Jersey were sadly no more. I couldn't understand why, but I intended to find out.

I couldn't help remembering how happy I'd been during the past year - the joys of rambling through dappled lanes alive with birdsong and insect buzzes, the contented lowing of

Jersey's gentle-eyed cows, and the languid lunches with friends at quaint country pubs. But those days seemed just a dream.

Then there'd been the golden days swimming in secluded bays hidden by towering cliffs, the endless blue skies above, laughter and love – all just a memory now.

Autumn had come and gone, with long country walks through lanes thickly carpeted with leaves, or along perilous narrow cliffs high above the undulating sea. Then we'd return home wind-blown, red-cheeked and deliriously happy – or so I'd innocently believed.

The cottage, cosily warmed by a glowing fire in the granite fireplace, had been the centre of my life throughout the winter, and while the winds howled and the seas raged, and long nights blanketed the island in darkness, I'd felt safe and remote from the world - except for James's growing aloofness. Often he was home late and I would stare out into the lonely dark, watching for the cheerful glow of his headlights and wondering what had kept him and why we hadn't made love for months.

When winter gave way to a damp, bright spring, and the garden was ablaze with bluebells, snowdrops and masses of daffodils, I discovered James's secret.

He'd left his mobile phone next to the bed while fetching firewood from the shed. It rang suddenly, and because James was down at the bottom of the garden, I decided to answer it. I knew he didn't like me taking his calls but I thought it could be important. As I picked it up, and before I could speak, I heard a voice – a woman's voice - and what I heard made my blood run cold.

"James- I know the bitch is there, so I'll be quick. Same place and don't be late. I can't wait to..."

The phone fell from my nerveless fingers. There was no mistaking what the call was about. I felt dizzy, and my heart pounded painfully in my chest. It couldn't be true! Yet all the signs were there. Everything fell into place – the excuses, the hours away supposedly at the office, James's indifference, and his lost, far-away expression.

Anger and mad fury threatened to take over. I was tempted to rush outside and face him, but I stopped and stood still, breathing slowly to calm my wild thoughts and shaking hands. I then realised I had to do something about it. But what? It was no use shouting and accusing him. He would just storm out and I'd be left to pick up the pieces. I couldn't bear the thought of leaving Jersey. I loved it passionately and couldn't picture myself anywhere else, especially without James. I had to try and win James back – woo him, make him realise his mistake, make him love me again. I prayed it wasn't too late.

James was unaware that I knew his secret, and during the next weeks I was as loving and caring as possible, even though my heart was breaking.

"What's come over you, Lucy? You're all over me and I wish you'd stop fawning."

"I'm just trying to show you how much I care, my darling. You seem so worried about work; I'm just trying to help."

"Well don't. I hate being smothered. I've a lot on my mind."

And I have too, I'd told myself silently.

I began to look at him with new eyes. He'd become irritated at all I did and said, and I was painfully aware of the way his lip curled when he spoke to me. His voice was no longer soft and loving, but harsh and snappy, with a sarcastic nastiness which hurt me to the very core.

"Let's get out into the fresh air, darling," I coaxed one day after a silent lunch where it was obvious he wasn't going to be pleasant. "It's so close in here, so confining. Let's go somewhere where we can talk and let the wind blow the cobwebs away. We need to, James. It's only fair that I know what's happening to us. I know - let's go to Grosnez Castle again, just like the very first time you took me there."

At first he shook me off impatiently, pretending there was nothing the matter, then to my surprise, he reluctantly agreed. "I suppose it's a good idea. We do need to talk, but not here."

It was a cold, blustery winter's day. Icy fingers of wind snatched at our coats and whipped at our scarves as we made our way along the path to the castle.

"Let's walk for a bit, James. I need to clear my head and breathe the fresh air."

James strode beside me, his head down against the wind. We'd wandered along the cliff edge away from the castle and towards the deep chasm. I'd noticed there was not another soul to be seen. We were the only ones braving the fierce wind in that wild, desolate spot.

"I've always loved it here, James," I chatted brightly. "It excites my imagination. I often walk to the edge of the cliff and gaze at the other islands and wonder if they can see us looking at them."

He merely grunted and pulled his coat and scarf closer. I then stopped and turned to face him.

"I know there's someone else, James. I'm not a fool. I wish you'd been open with me and not left me to work out why you don't love me anymore."

"I thought I did love you in my own way, Lucy, but you don't understand how much strain I've been under. I've made some bad business mistakes, and I'm afraid that before long they'll be discovered and then I'll be in deep trouble."

My heart seemed to stop still and I gasped in horror. Surely James hadn't been fiddling the books or - I had a sudden frightening thought – was actually stealing? I held out my arms and hugged him close. "But surely we can work this out together...?" I began.

But he angrily shook me off. "I can't. Nothing will help. Michelle and I ...we've made a plan."

"I suppose Michelle's my rival," I began to cry softly. "Your lover."

James nodded, his face bleak. "We've made plans. She can help me. So you see, Lucy, you must leave Jersey. Go away. There's nothing here for you now. It was all a big mistake. Go back to your family."

Sobbing, I flung myself into his arms and staggered forwards. I then pushed him as hard as I could. James

37

stumbled, lost his footing, and was unable to save himself. He pitched forward over the edge of the cliff and plummeted towards the waiting rocks below. His terrified screams were drowned by shrieking gulls wheeling high in the sky above. I crept to the edge and peered over as far as I dared. All I could see was the angry sea pounding greedily at the rocks below.

The plane from Jersey flies serenely over a turquoise sea. I'm almost blinded by the bright sun, so I turn my head away from the window and glance down at the handcuffs on my wrist and at the impassive face of the guard beside me.

"You'll get life for this, you know. That's what happens to murderers like you," she mutters.

I hang my head. Grosnez had taken my love, and now it is too late for tears.

LIBERATING JAMIE

MARLEEN HACQUOIL

Not famous for riding her horse to school on the Canadian prairies or for publishing a novel about a Jersey-born novelist, Elinor Glyn.

Liberating Jamie – By Marleen Hacquoil

It was the yellow month. Clarrie always thought of May that way. The yellow broom was competing with the gorse for space on the hillsides, some rogue daffodils were still bordering the cotils, and the sun was doing its best to bring on the main crop potatoes. This particular day in May had a special glitter because Dad had come down from the hayloft yesterday night with a broad grin on his face - he always spent six o'clock in the hayloft because that's where the radio was hidden - and he'd told the whole family, and not in a whisper either, that the Prime Minister, Mr. Churchill, had said the dear Channel Islands were to be liberated.

"What's liberated mean?" Clarrie had asked.

"Clarence, my son," Dad had answered, "that means them Germans has got to git off our island and leave us in peace once again."

"Does that mean we'll have more food to eat?" Lizzie had asked. She was only five and small for her age, but then none of the Ahiers was tall or wide for that matter.

Dad had looked at Mum and Mum had looked at Dad, in that special way they had, and Dad had said that maybe soon there'd be lots to eat. If the potato crop was good.

"I want sweeties," Lizzie had whined, and Mum had patted her head.

"Not good for you, my lamb, they rot your teeth. But there will be some, bye and bye."

Clarrie wanted to rush out right then and tell Jamie that the Germans were going and there was going to be sweeties, but he thought better of it. He'd had to be extra careful for years now about Jamie. If Dad or Mum had found out that he was sharing his food with a friend they'd have been mad as all heck. Dad already said that Clarrie was soft in the head. At twelve Clarrie was not much bigger than he'd been at nine, and that was when he'd found Jamie in the henhouse stealing eggs. Except there weren't any eggs to steal and the chickens had been gathered up and taken into the loft where they were put in barrels for the night. That way the Germans or the slave workers wouldn't get them when they broke in.

Young Clarrie had stood stock still there in the gloom when he saw the figure raking through the straw in the hens' boxes. He was scared but he was also fascinated because he'd never seen anyone so thin or so dirty. The figure saw him and froze. They had eyed each other, transfixed. This was no German, Clarrie knew, because he wore no uniform, just an assortment of rags. He didn't seem much older than Clarrie. The scarecrow had smiled when the shock of being discovered wore off, and put a finger to his lips. Clarrie's mind was in a tizz. He knew he ought to call his Dad, but he also knew his Dad would chase the boy away or turn him over to the Germans.

"You're a slave worker, aren't you?" The young man had only shrugged, then pointed to himself and said, "Jaime."

"Haimey? Jamie, maybe. You're hungry." Clarrie knew what it was like to be hungry. Maybe he could help this young prisoner. "Stay here," he'd said, putting a finger to his own lips. He'd backed out the door and closed it behind him, then tiptoed into the house and into the pantry where Mum kept the bread in a stone crock. Carefully lifting the lid, he drew out the half-loaf and wondered how much he could take without it being noticed. Then, with a hunk of it in his pocket, he slipped back to the henhouse, picking up a windfall apple from the ground as he went. Bearing his gifts he entered the gloom of the henhouse. Nothing moved. Where was the slave worker?

"Jamie," he'd whispered urgently. The straw in the corner rustled and Jaime's blackened face emerged. "Here, I've brought you something." He thrust his offerings towards the stricken figure. Jaime's huge eyes took in the bread and the apple, and tears began to trace patterns down his cheeks. He stretched his hand forward and Clarrie saw that the fingers looked much like the claws of chickens, all knuckles and nails.

Jamie would be his secret, Clarrie decided. No one, not even Lizzie was to know about Clarrie's friend. He'd found a place in one of the unused barns where Jamie could hide and any scrap of food that didn't go to the pig was pilfered and delivered to the young man. When he could disappear without being missed, Clarrie would join his friend and talk to him, although he couldn't understand a word Jamie said, and Jamie probably couldn't understand him. Because of this incomprehension, Clarrie felt free to tell Jamie everything.

When Dad came down the stairs that May day and announced the Liberation, Mum and Dad hugged one another and little Lizzie, and put their arms around Clarrie, but he didn't feel the way they did. What would happen now, he wondered, would Jamie leave and go home, would he lose his best friend, the quietest friend he had in the world?

"Sorry, son, but Mum and I are going into town to see our troops land at the harbour, and there's no sense taking Lizzie 'cause she's too young and she'll just get tired and trampled on. You'll have to stay home and watch her, but we'll tell you all about it when we get back. You don't mind, do you?" And Clarrie didn't mind because, of course, he wanted to share the news with Jamie. It would have been fun to see the British troops land and the Germans be marched away, or whatever would happen to them. Maybe they'd shoot them.

As soon as Dad had hitched Queenie to the cart and he and Mum had driven down the road, Lizzie had clasped Clarrie's hand and begged him to play hide and seek with her. "Okay, Lizzie," he said. "You count to 50 - can you do that? - and I'll hide somewhere in the yard and you come find me." Then he'd gone to the old barn where Jamie was, and waited.

"Clarrie, where are you, I give up," wailed Lizzie some minutes later. Her brother opened the door a crack and called to her. "I'm here, Lizzie, don't get upset. Come here, I want to show you something." Lizzie came running, then tripping through the weeds that surrounded the derelict stone outbuilding. "That's not fair, Clarrie, you were supposed to hide in the yard." Clarrie took her hand and bent down to whisper in her ear. "I've got a surprise for you, Lizzie. Come and meet my friend Jamie." He led the little girl through the splintered wooden doorway into the dark of the barn.

"Here he is, Lizzie, this is Jamie, my best friend in the whole world."

Lizzie could see only old straw and cobwebs, but she looked where Clarrie was pointing to some old rags spread out on the floor. At the edge of the rags she saw a foot, two feet, and some distance above them, a skull. She put her hands to her mouth and screamed as loud as she could scream.

"It's okay, Lizzie, he won't hurt you, this is Jamie, and he's been in this place for months, and I've been looking after him. Haven't I, Jamie?" But Jamie didn't answer. He'd been quiet for ever so long, months, maybe years. He'd stopped eating way back, but he still listened to Clarrie when he came to call. And Clarrie liked it that way. He hoped the Liberation wasn't going to spoil all that.

V FOR VICTORY

GEORGINA TROY

Georgina Troy writes contemporary women's fiction based in Jersey. Her Jersey Scene series is published by Accent Press.

V for Victory – By Georgina Troy

"Shush." Katherine raised one of her annoyingly slender index fingers up to her mouth. "They're outside."

Monica carefully dusted the flour from her hands not wishing to waste any and watched it fall on to the worn wooden table. She resisted telling her sister to stop bossing her about, but the fear of why uninvited visitors were now standing outside the door silenced her.

"Why do you think they've stopped?" she whispered, listening intently for any footsteps. She could hear her own breathing and wondered if the Nazis at the door could too.

Both girls stood heads tilted to one side in an effort to hear any movement.

Unable to bear the suspense another moment, Monica crept over to the window and slowly pulled back the edge of the heavy lace curtain. Spotting a lone German straightening his cap, she jumped back when he glanced in her direction. She nodded towards the door. "There's only one."

"What's he doing out there?" Katherine's eyes widened. "Do you think he knows about…?"

He banged loudly on the front door and both girls gasped.

"You answer it," said Monica, pushing her sister ahead of her."

"No, you."

"Open this door, immediately," a voice, deep and clipped, demanded from outside.

Monica took a deep breath. Not wishing to give their neighbours a show, she scowled at her sister. "Coward," she said, elbowing passed Katherine and pushing down on the door handle before opening the door. "Yes?" she asked, determined to keep an aloof expression on her face despite her knees shaking under her skirt.

"I wish to come in to your home," said the blond soldier who, Monica presumed, couldn't be much older than her. He looked barely twenty, although far more confident than she ever felt.

"Why?" she asked glancing around the street and seeing several curtains dropping into place. Nosy buggers.

"I am told you are bakers," he said frowning. "I wish to purchase bread."

Katherine turned to get one of their precious loaves from the worktop at the back of the room, but Monica reached back and grabbed her sister's wrist. She shook her head at the soldier. "We don't have any bread available," she lied. "There are so few ingredients now."

"But, Mon?"

She ignored her sister's confusion. Katherine had always been a little dim when it came to telling fibs and was no doubt terrified about lying to this man, but Monica didn't care.

The officer laughed. "Nonsense, you have flour on your apron and your hands. You will bake me bread and I will wait for it."

Katherine shrugged off her sister's grip and left the room.

Monica watched her go before looking back at the soldier. She was irritated by his demands, but aware she wasn't in a position to argue. She stepped back to let him in trying to curb her nervousness and watched as the soldier pulled out a seat and sat down facing her.

She stared at him in disbelief. "You're going to sit and watch me make it?"

He nodded. "I do not wish for you to make any unexpected, how you say, additions?" He laughed at his own joke.

If only I had the guts to give poisoning a go, she thought, forcing a smile and picking up her dough to continue kneading it.

The soldier spotted the photo of their parents on the sideboard and pointed to it. "This is your parents, ja?"

Monica nodded. She wished her dad would hurry up and get home, or maybe it would be better if he stayed away until this chap had left them.

"He is where?" the solder asked. "I believe I might have seen him before."

Here goes, thought Monica. She opened her mouth to speak when Katherine walked back into the room, placing a glass of water down heavily onto the table in front of the fair-haired stranger.

"He's at work," she snapped, glancing at Monica nervously.

"And his work is what?"

"Stonemason," both girls said in unison.

"He's working on the gates at the bottom of the Sunshine Hotel," Katherine added.

"One of the Feld Kommandant's headquarters?"

"Yes," Monica bit back a retort. It wasn't her place to insult these unpredictable jailers of theirs, their father had pleaded with them many times to watch every word they said.

"I will look at his work when I am next there."

I do hope not too closely, thought Monica as she dropped the dough into the loaf tin. "He's very proud of what he does," she said, hoping he hadn't noticed Katherine's frightened expression.

"Right, this should be ready now. I'll put it in the oven and you can come back and collect it in about an hour if you want?"

He shook his head. "I'm not certain I can trust you."

Monica pulled a 'help me' face at her sister. She couldn't bear the thought of this man sitting in their kitchen for a moment longer than was necessary. He was the enemy. He may be similar in age to her and Katherine, however she was certain that was where the similarity between them ended.

"I've got an idea," Katherine said. "Why don't you make a sign, or something, on the top of the loaf before Mon puts it into the oven? That way you can tell it's not been tampered with and you can be sure it's the one you watched her make."

He glanced from one to the other of them thoughtfully and then rose to his feet. "Yes, this sounds acceptable."

He held out his hand and pointed to a sharp knife lying on the chopping board. Monica picked it up, her hand trembling as she handed it to him and watched as he cut various crosses into the puffy dough.

"This is good." He placed the knife back down on the table and stepped back. "I will return in one hour," he said, giving them a curt nod before leaving.

Both girls breathed a sigh of relief as soon as their front door closed behind him.

"Well done, Kat," Monica said. Taking a tea cloth, she carefully opened the oven door and placed the tin inside. "I thought he was going to sit there for the next hour."

"Never mind him," Katherine said frowning. "What's going to happen when he looks at those gates at the Kommandant's headquarters?"

50

"You were the one who told him about them?"

"I know," Katherine sighed. "If he discovers what's there Dad will be in terrible trouble."

"There's nothing we can do about it now."

"We have to tell Dad what happened. Maybe he can quickly redo his work."

"What work?" Their father stepped into the house, shutting the door and hanging his rucksack up on the nearby hook. He shrugged off his loose cotton jacket and draped it across the back of one of the chairs.

Monica took a deep breath. "Dad, we need to tell you something."

He sat down in his seat at the head of the table and listened as she explained about the soldier and accidentally telling him about the wall.

They waited while their father thought about this, before shaking his head and sighing.

"Do you think he'll notice it?" Katherine asked wrapping her arms around her waist and looking as if she was about to cry.

"Dad?" Monica felt for Katherine, but mostly for their father. If he was caught he'd probably be deported to Germany to one of those prison camps, or maybe shot like that young Frenchman, François Scornet, who'd arrived in the island believing it to be England. Panic coursed through her. How

51

could Katherine have been so stupid to mention the damn wall, she wondered.

"We'll just have to hope that he either forgets about it, or is too unobservant and misses it," he said. "There's nothing else we can do about it now."

The hour passed slowly, but Monica couldn't eliminate the feeling of foreboding that seemed to fill their small kitchen. Eventually she heard the unmistakeable sound of jackboots walking along the pavement. They stopped outside their back door and Katherine went to let the soldier in.

"Guten tag," he said, as if he was a friend simply visiting their home, not someone they had no choice but to allow inside. He nodded a greeting to their father, who simply glared back. The soldier looked over to Monica. "It is ready?"

"Yes," she said.

"Danke schön." She handed him the warm loaf. "This is for the ingredients."

"Oh, right," Monica said, taken aback when he dropped several coins into her palm.

She stared at the currency she'd come to hate, longing for the day these invaders left, pushing away the fear that it wouldn't be happening in a hurry. One day they would be able to use their own pennies and shillings again. One day, these noisy jackboots that seemed to vibrate their houses every time a group of German soldiers marched along the road in front of their terrace, would be gone and that day couldn't come soon enough as far as she was concerned.

She walked over to the door to show him out, but just as he reached the doorstep, he turned to their father. "I have seen the walls on which your daughters tell me you are working. I wish to know how you knew the Feld Kommandants' initials."

"I beg your pardon?"

Monica held her breath. She couldn't bear to listen to her father's reply.

"The 'Vs' you have incorporated into the pattern on the stones on each side of the gateposts, it is very clever. He will be pleased I think?" He narrowed his eyes. "How did you know his name?"

"Um," their father shook his head. "I believe he requested this for a surprise, but one that must not be discussed. Please do not mention it to anyone, I would hate for the secret to be discovered too soon."

"Of course," said the soldier, clicking his heels together and nodding at their father. "I will leave you now. Guten tag."

Monica waited until the door was closed before exhaling once again. She felt faint with relief, gripping the top of the kitchen table as she gathered herself. "Do you think he believed you, Dad?"

Their father grinned. "He believed me all right. It only goes to show that being gullible is an international affliction."

"How many 'V' signs have been inserted into the streets and walls of the island do you think?" Monica asked, proud of her father's secret rebellion against their invaders.

"I've no idea," he shrugged. "I got the idea from another stonemason, Joseph, who's cleverly included one in the Royal Square that the Germans haven't discovered yet despite it being several feet in length."

"I'll have to look for it next time I'm walking through the square." She tried to picture it among the paving stones where most people walked at some point during their week. "It must give you a sense of satisfaction to know locals can see the 'victory' signs while the Nazis seem oblivious to them.

"It does," he agreed smiling. "His is hidden in plain sight; clever man. Best place to hide anything," he said pulling his daughters into a hug.

REMEMBER?

DAFF NOËL

Daff was born during the German Occupation of the island and has become an established writer of local fact and fiction.

Remember? – By Daff Noël

Katya smiled as she looked around the large sitting room of Les Hirondelles in St. Martin. The elderly residents had taken some time to settle into their favourite armchairs but for once there had been no argument or discussion as to who should sit where. The afternoon session of entertainment by the local musical duo had become very popular and though some would drift off to sleep, others would sing along or in the very least show that they were enjoying the music by a tapping of the hand or just movement of the fingers – as in the case of Ada Cory who used to be a music teacher. Satisfied that all would be well for the next half hour or so she made her way down the passage towards the kitchen where she hoped the chef Jon would carry out his promise to show her how to make Jersey Wonders. They were different from any other cake she'd either seen or eaten so she wanted to take some home on her next visit to Poland.

As she passed the open doorway of room twenty-three she took a step back to call into the room, "It's a pity you won't go in to hear the music, Marie. You would really enjoy it. Are you sure you wouldn't like me to take you?"

But Marie Dessain, staring out of the window with her back towards the door made no response, indeed she remained without moving for some time after Katya had passed. It was only when the rendering of the song 'We'll Meet Again' drifted up the passage and gradually penetrated her brain that she began to rock backwards and forwards.

The music had re-awakened a memory of being back in one of the dim, musty old rooms of the Museum when William had just broken the devastating news that he and his mother were leaving the island for Australia on the £10 immigration scheme. They would be six weeks on a liner, he told her excitedly, and then housed in a hostel until he and his mother found work after which they would buy a house.

"Aw! Don't cry!" he'd said when he saw the tears run down her cheeks. "We'll meet again." And then as if to cheer her up he had taken her in his arms, singing the number softly.

"We'll meet again,

Don't know where, don't know when,

But I know we'll meet again some sunny day ..."

Marie was the only child of Thomas and Avril Billot, the caretakers of the Museum in Pier Road. During her growing years she had become very familiar with the ancient exhibits while helping her parents carefully dust each one when cleaning from room to room on a monthly basis. They were mostly boring objects brought together to make an equally boring display, but the reconstructed old kitchen, situated on the ground floor at the back of the building in Caledonian Place, was different. This always captured Marie's imagination causing her mind's eye to see a real family living there: a mother, father, three children under six and a baby in the cot by the fire, with a smiling granny, dressed in black from head-to-foot, watching over it. They became the constant but imaginary companions of the shy child who stood alone in the playground of Halkett Place each school day, unable to make friends.

Nobody ever seemed to notice her, she seemed invisible to everyone. That was until the magical evening her parents locked the heavy doors of the Museum and took her across the road to attend a concert at the Pier Road Mission. Throughout her life thereafter, for as long as she could remember, that evening remained with her as the day she made her first real friend, and that friend was William.

Everyone who lived in Pier Road seemed to be involved with the Mission in one way or another. Situated up a narrow lane exactly opposite the Caledonian Steps it was not only their place of simple worship under the guiding hand of Captain Blake, but the community centre where they all got together for amusements such as concerts, dances and picnics. William and his widowed mother had recently moved into the two attic rooms of number seven, and the large Butcher family who occupied the rest of the house had taken them along to the concert.

It was customary to chat over tea and cake after such events, and Avril, who was serving the teas, was delighted to recognise the newcomer as her old school friend, Jeanne Dessain. The two youngsters stood aside while the mothers chatted away, Marie looking at the floor while William eyed her curiously until suddenly he whispered, "I'm going to get some cake. Do you want some?" She looked up but seeing that he was already making his way towards the table laden with cakes and biscuits returned her gaze to the floor. Then suddenly she felt herself being pulled by the wrist as he urged "Come on! They'll be all eaten if we don't hurry!"

With their mothers' old friendship renewed, the two began to spend a great deal of time together, especially after Avril discovered that William had to be left alone while Jeanne worked until late in the chip shop on the bottom corner of the road. She insisted he had his evening meal with them on the evenings his mother worked, and when Jeanne protested, saying she couldn't take advantage of such kindness, she suggested he help with the Museum as payment.

William was a keen worker but when alone with Marie confessed that he found the exhibits in the upper rooms boring. How could she bear to have such dull things around her every day? He asked. She took him down to the kitchen and timidly told him all she imagined. She expected him to sneer but instead he looked at her for a long time before saying, "You know Marie, if what you imagine could be made to actually happen, if somehow those old objects in the rooms upstairs could be made to talk, museums would be wonderful places, not dull and boring as they are now." She adored him from that moment on.

The years passed with the pair visiting the various places of interest in the island whenever they could, but mostly they would walk the town, investigating any old and empty house, talking to the inhabitants of tiny cottages in yards such as those in Hue Street, making copious notes for the book William said he would write one day. It was an interest which, Marie thought, would consume them forever.

But it was shortly after her fourteenth birthday that William broke the awful news.

Marie sobbed now, as she did back then when she leant out over the land tie at the end of the Albert Pier, waving until the boat sailed out of sight behind the Castle.

Hands gripped her shoulders in an effort to still her but she shrugged them away to rock more furiously. A white handkerchief approached her face and a man's voice said, "Come on, I don't know what all this crying is about but let's dry those tears."

She smacked the hand away.

"William! I want William!" she cried. Then she stopped rocking to look the man in the face. "William left me to go to Australia."

"And I came back and married you!" William Dessain said with a sigh. "Fifty-six years and you can't remember any of it." He thought of reminding her yet again of the many changes in the way local history was now presented, just as she had imagined all those years ago but as he dabbed away her tears the vacant look in her eyes re-appeared so he felt silent. He had been advised to continue talking to her as if she heard, as if she understood, but what was there to talk about now? He thought miserably.

He looked up as Joe and Joan Le Masurier came into the room.

"Hello Will," said Joe, shaking his hand. "Thought we'd pop in while we were here." He looked down and seeing the unresponsive Marie asked, "How is she?" The couple continued to eye Marie silently as Will replied that she was 'fine'.

"Great news about the Foot properties in Dumaresq Street," Joe, a staunch fellow member of Jersey Heritage said. "We'll need to work on the fund-raising but it'll be another great day when we see those finally restored, especially the old sign, eh?"

Will smiled broadly as he nodded in reply. He and Marie had admired the sign advertising His Masters Voice gramophones for so many years and had despaired at the way it had been left to wear away.

He could hardly wait for his friends to leave. There was so much that he had to talk to Marie about after all.

UN BAÎSI ÎMPÈRMÎNS

COLIN LEVER

Colin Lever is a Freelance writer of non-fiction, education texts.
Author of *La Chaire, beyond the garden gate.*

Un baîsi împèrmîns (A Forbidden Kiss) – By Colin Lever

The door is slightly ajar and I can see him going about his business. Now he is in shot and he glances in my direction. I look away immediately, waiting a few seconds before peering to see if he is still there. Our eyes meet briefly and then he is gone. I am disappointed.

The next day I see him again, but a little later on. As I serve a customer he passes by the shop a little slower, or so it seems. He pauses to look inside, to catch my eye, or so I presume. The old woman is an irritation.

"I will be glad when this war is over," she witters.

I ignore her. My attention is elsewhere. I can't help but feel sorry for him as he swelters under the unforgiving, midday sun. It is so much cooler in the shop.

"You can't get hold of anything," she continues.

"Um," is all I say as she hands the money over.

I look at him dreamily, taken in by his boyish features and that gaze.

"Excuse me." The spell is broken.

"Pardon?" My tone is rude.

Reluctantly I am compelled to look away and deal with the old bag.

"You have not given me my change," she complains, her hand held out in anticipation.

"I am so sorry," I say as I fumble in the till, trying to work out how much I owe her.

She huffs, grudgingly, as she checks her change.

"You can never be too careful these days," she snipes as she makes for the door. The barb passes over my head. I am more concerned with him. I lean this way and that trying to see past her but he has gone. Wistfully I return to my chores. That evening my sleep is disturbed, interrupted by wishful thinking, dreaming of what might be. At last there is light in all of the grey that is the occupation.

It is morning and I awake early, anticipation coursing through my veins. I button up my blouse incorrectly and for the life of me I cannot get the zip on my skirt to shift. Everything seems to be playing hide and seek, my make-up, my hand bag...

"Mum have you moved my shoes?"

"They will be where you left them," she says with a sigh.

I rush out of the door, my coat refusing to comply as it is caught by the breeze. In my haste, I stumble on the cobbles. I am more concerned with looking to see if he is in the vicinity.

"You're early." Mr Maier observes.

"Not really." I dismiss his comment, my mind on more pressing issues.

"Would you sort out the magazines?"

"Of course."

My eagerness to oblige makes him pause and turn his head briefly to look at me from atop the ladders. The shop doorbell tinkles and I jump up expectantly, dusting down my skirt and knees. Before I get a chance to turn I hear their voices, the language is German. The realisation makes me hesitate. I am in limbo, standing facing the wall, statuesque. I can feel their eyes looking me up and down. I am excited and intimidated in equal measure. Mr Maier comes to my rescue.

"I will serve these gentlemen." He is always so polite.

As they are being served I can hear them talking, turning to leer at me as they speak. They are boorish and loud. I do not speak German but I know they are talking about me. Anything in a skirt! The laughter in their voices is demeaning and I wish that they would leave.

One of them steps in my direction and my heart flutters. I am afraid. I keep my eyes firmly on the task in hand. I cannot help but see his polished ankle boots and the grey-green of his trousers. He speaks to me, his voice is gentle and matter of fact but I ignore him. He speaks again and once more I rebuff him. There is an impasse until finally, he gets the message. The doorbell signifies their exit so I dare to look up. My heart drops as I see him leaving the shop. I look over to Mr Maier, he is disappointed. He is a wise old sage and can read me like a book. He says nothing, returning to his precious shelves.

I wait, hoping that I see the soldier again. There is a pit in my stomach that I cannot appease. I try and concentrate but it is hard to focus when your mind wanders so. As the days pass my disappointment turns to relief. Common sense prevails and I am coming round to the opinion that to even think of fraternising with the enemy is a mistake.

Today it is my responsibility to shut up shop. I give the place the once over before leaving. I lock the door top and bottom.

"Good evening, Fraulein."

I visibly jump and I have to stifle the need to scream for fear of alerting passersby. He is standing right next to me and for a brief moment I feel no guilt, no shame, just elation that he is here, by my side. How good it feels to be wanted. I come to my senses and try to take a step backwards but I cannot, he has me pinned to the door. Like a true gentleman, he recognises my discomfort and retreats to a safe distance. His smile is reassuring and I reciprocate.

"I am sorry that I startled you."

Is that shyness I detect in him, how sweet?

I want to speak to him but should I? I have been raised to display good manners. It is an anathema to me to be knowingly rude but this is different isn't it? I must not speak to the Bosch, they are our adversaries.

'Speak only when you are spoken to.'

That's what my Papa told me, so there is no harm in talking, surely? To parley is to court censure. All it would take is for

66

someone; even a stranger, to see us together and I would be undone.

But is it wrong to deny myself a little fun in this time of austerity? He is so tall and handsome. Those Germanic features, chiselled from the mountains of Bavaria, the blond hair the blue eyes that look into your very soul, are so striking. How can I resist? And why should I?

"May I walk with you?" he asked respectfully.

"No thank you." I am horrified by my curt reply.

I set off at a pace, catching him unawares. My heart is pounding in my breast. I know I am blushing and my head feels like it is about to explode. I cannot think straight. He catches up with me, his long legs eating up the space in no time.

"Please may I speak with you?" he entreats, matching me stride for stride yet careful not to turn his head to face me, lest people should know that we are having a conversation.

"I'd prefer it if you did not." The haughtiness in my voice almost makes me giggle.

"I only want to talk with you," he pleads as we separate to avoid oncoming pedestrians.

Should I stop and hear what he has to say? I mean, what harm can it do? Perhaps if I could find somewhere private where we could just sit, away from prying eyes? I scan either side of the street for a likely place. This is all so clandestine.

"Cigarette?" He could sense my resistance faltering, I was sure of it.

"No thank you...I don't smoke!"

I felt the urge to giggle once more, and was that a skip in my step?

He continues to shadow me as we slalom down the narrow pavement. I turn quickly into a blind alley, disappearing into the gloom. I almost lose him but he too, hesitantly, gives pursuit. The silence is expectant. Our lips meet and we embrace for what seems like an age. My heart races and I have butterflies. I am as close to ecstasy as I have ever been. I wish this feeling would last forever. We come up for air. I take the opportunity to divest myself of his attentions, escaping back into the morass, leaving him clutching thin air and confused.

Exhilarated by our forbidden kiss, I run like the wind. It is as if the very hounds of hell are snapping at my heels. I lose count of how many people I bump into as I dodge and weave down King Street. Adrenalin fuels my whole body, giving me the strength to run on and on. I dare not look back in case he is giving chase, for I know that if he is pursuing me I would not have the strength to resist. Eventually I feel my legs starting to ache. I cannot get enough oxygen into my lungs and so I have to stop. Tentatively I look behind me, panting, half expecting him to be upon me but he is nowhere to be seen. I am saddened to see that he does not have the desire to follow but I am, equally, relieved that he chose not to. I have crossed a line and the realisation of my impulsive actions starts to sink in.

Exhausted, I walk slowly home, nervously looking over my shoulder, just in case. I am wracked with guilt and I avoid anything but a cursory acknowledgment once the front door closes behind me. I nip upstairs and shut the bedroom door. I have sanctuary. The anxieties kick in. What happens if he turns up at the shop? Mr Maier is sure to see right through me. How can I possibly face either of them? How long will it take before others get wind of my indulgence? His friends are bound to find out. I bet he is bragging to them right now. Oh what have I done? I will be ostracised, or worse. How could I have been so naive? I have brought disgrace on my family. Maybe I should take the day off and feign sickness, perhaps two days or even a week. The longer I stay away the better. Maybe I should just run away and be damned. But there is nowhere to go.

Today I am filled with trepidation. I feel nauseous but I am resolute and the decent thing to do is to face the music. As I fear, soldiers enter the shop just after lunch. There is a sharp exchange of words between them and Mr Maier, this is so unusual. They unceremoniously drag him from behind the counter shoving him with their rifle butts. The old man stumbles and moans under the blows. I run to his aid but blocking my way is the soldier. Our eyes meet briefly. I entreat. Where once there was a connection, an adolescent passion, now there is just a look of cold steel. He looks right through me, as if we never were, like I am some contagion. The revulsion I see brings me to tears. I try to push past him but it he is too strong for me. Mr Maier is handcuffed before being caste into the street, to the horror of the passersby. I, too, am jostled out of the door. I trip and find myself sitting on the dirty cobbles beside the old man. It is as if we are in disgrace. We both watch as the soldier dips a paintbrush and writes the word Juden in large white letters across the window, followed by a Star of David below.

My desolation is complete for now I know my fate. I, too, am a child of Abraham.

OUELLE EST GAÛCHIE

JAN CASTON

Writer/Screenwriter/Film Producer Jan Caston specialises in family entertainment. She is currently writing a series of books of more adventures based on the characters from the children's' film *Who Killed Nelson Nutmeg?*

Ouelle Est Gaûchie – By Jan Caston

Our conversation opened in that typical Jersey way. "I know you," said the old woman coming up too close to my face. She spoke very loudly and invaded my personal space. I took a step backwards. I didn't recognise her. "You're the youngest girl Houillebecq. You're one of Ernie's."

"Sorry. I'm not local." She took another quizzical look before she perfunctorily turned her back on me. I'd confessed I wasn't Jersey born. With those four polite little words, I seemingly sealed her opinion of me.

Eighteen embroiderers from the Parish of St Lawrence attended the meeting that evening. Even before we were split into three teams of six, Maman had worked the room and found out who everyone else was. She was an old woman with a very long memory.

She listened to Wayne Audrain, the designer of the Occupation Tapestry, with great deference; well, at that point I assumed it was deference; after all he was the man who had brilliantly brought the community project to life. Later I was to find out that all men, to Maman, are less than mere mortals. Maman believed the way you dealt with men was to flatter, tolerate or dismiss. Maman did a lot of dismissing. She was one very hard, old, Jersey Bean!

"There's an awful lot of work to get done to complete this on time," said Jane, our administrator. "We're one of the later Parishes to start. All twelve panels have to be finished by Christmas 1994 so they can be hung ready for the fiftieth anniversary of the Liberation the next year." That gave us about eighteen months to finish our panel - School and Work. It was going to be no mean feat.

My heart sank as the arrangements were discussed. I'd been delighted to have been selected to work on the tapestry but hadn't thought any further than that. How was I going to fit in such a time pressured regular requirement with my job? Could I back out now?

Too late, I thought and took down notes. The canvas had already been sewn onto its frame ready for the first stitch. Filling an entire wall was the paper template. Just like painting with numbers, each block of colour had been given its Appletons Crewel Wool reference. We would be using two hundred and seventy different shades of fifty two different colours to fill the seven and a half million stitches on our panel. The project was huge.

Maman made a fuss even before we started. "If there are two hundred and seventy shades, we're going to need more of those boxes." Regimentally organised on shelves were about a hundred boxes containing the wools. "Some colours are only used very little," Jane explained. Maman didn't listen. "And where are the needles? I like to work with my own needles."

"We provide new needles. We can't risk damaging the canvas. You can bring your own embroidery scissors, if you must... as long as I check them first."

Maman gave Jane a black glare and moved into position centre top of the canvas. She put her hand firmly over one of the framed scenes. It was immediately to the left of the largest figure, a German soldier in uniform. "I won't work on the Kraut, so don't even ask me." It was obvious what she wanted to work on. It was the prettiest scene showing a couple collecting vraic in front of La Rocco Tower with people long line fishing behind them. Of course, she got it.

Was she going to be trouble! I hung back and waited to be allocated my work place. Jane consulted her notes. "I need one of you up there," she said and pointed to the top left of the canvas. It wasn't yet clear what that area depicted as the canvas was stitched to a frame the size of a large refectory table, then rolled inwards horizontally so the middle section could be worked first. We would be working with one arm above the canvas and one below. Most of the scene was currently obscured within the roll.

Maman beat Jane to her decision. "Have her," she commanded and pointed at me. "Ouelle est gaûchie". Some ladies laughed. I don't speak Jersey French and because I hadn't a clue what she'd said, I heard only her fierce tone.

My blood boiled. I felt I'd just been given the short straw and assumed it was because I was the stranger. "Yes. Perfect. You do this bit…," said Jane pushing me round directly in front of it. I would be working sitting at an angle alongside Maman. There would also be a leg of the frame in my way. "Perfect" was not the word that sprung immediately to my mind.

"… but you'll have to be constantly vigilant about the tension," Jane finished and moved away. I couldn't be sure if

74

that was a needlework instruction or a warning. Maman grinned smarmily and eyeballed me. I decided not to ask.

Instead I checked the template to see what I would be working on. It was a silhouette very reminiscent of an Edmund Blampied painting of a man driving a horse and cart home to a farmstead at dusk. I would have three colours to work with and nearly seventy two square inches to complete. Damn Maman! She got the prettiest panel and I got something black, orange and red, but mostly black. Why had I ever volunteered?

As worked progressed, every session, Maman dominated any conversation; but there's a rhythm to working tapestry that soothes. I turned a deaf ear and decided to let my needle do my talking. I had a plan. Once I'd finished the first block of black, I would go in early to start the orange on my own. An hour of peace and quiet and a different challenge were to be my treats, but when the day arrived, I wasn't the first there. Aurélie was already working the schoolmistress's dress in lilac wool.

"I'm having trouble with her white buttons," she said without looking up. I leant over her. "They're round and Basket Weave Tent Stitch is essentially oblong."

"Could they be offset?" I suggested and she offered me a needle already threaded with white. I sat down beside her and did some trial stitches.

"That's not your place!" We both jumped. Maman had come in without us hearing.

"This lady's just...," Aurélie started, but got rudely interrupted. "Get back to your black. You were given that job to do," Maman sharply ordered me.

I wasn't prepared to cause an argument with an old and crotchety woman. I handed the needle threaded with white back to Aurélie and went to collect my own wools. The other ladies arrived and started working. I could see Aurélie was still seething. It was obvious they could sense the atmosphere too.

"I was here in the Occupation as well, you know." Aurélie eventually broke the silence. "You weren't the only one who went through it."

"No need to talk about it, then, is there?" growled Maman and, for some unknown reason, eyeballed me.

Across the tapestry Aurélie tenderly touched Maman's hand. It was as much as Maman could do to turn her eyes back to her. "It'll be fifty years by the time we get this finished. Don't you think it's about time you put all that resentment behind you?"

We all stopped working. Maman went puce. "You've always made out you were better than the rest of us, Aurélie Beaugeard, just because you did that damned underground newspaper," she retorted.

"Was that you?" one of the other ladies asked Aurélie, genuinely surprised.

"Only because I'd just finished at secretarial school and could use my shorthand to take down the nightly news from the BBC."

"But you kept the rest of us going. With the wireless banned, we were desperate to get any news out of England. You risked your life doing that!"

"It was so exciting to outwit the Jerries!" said Aurélie, grinning broadly.

"I was only a little "un," said the lady working the German in his green uniform. "I don't mind doing you, do I, Hans?" she said stroking his half completed chest. "I'd like to think you were the kind German who put food under the gatepost for me every morning after I started school. You saved me from starving."

Maman couldn't hold it any longer. She exploded in a rapid and angry stream of Jérriais. We were all shocked at the vehemence. Only Aurélie knew the patois and she spoke back firmly in English. "Yes, they were tyrants, Maman. Yes, I know your parents were interned at Bad Wurzach, but they did come back alive."

"Didn't stop looters robbing our furniture! I know what family took it to burn!"

"People were desperate! It made them look after their own. Everyone lost five years of their lives. No one knew who to trust. We lost faith in Britain because they abandoned us when we needed them the most; though His Majesty and Mr Churchill did try to put that right afterwards. But we never lost ourselves, Maman. We never stopped being Jersey folk. We got through it somehow."

"My sister lost the baby she was carrying!"

We all went quiet. Maman's cheeks were mottled. I was getting concerned.

"I didn't think your sister was here during the Occupation," said Aurélie.

"She talked her way onto the last boat of evacuees going to Weymouth so she could be nearer her husband when the baby came. He was off fighting with the R.A.F. She lost the baby in the middle of the Channel in a storm covered only by a tarpaulin on top of an old open-topped coal barge. She was seven months gone. And then her husband got shot down too."

No one spoke. Maman's breathing had become spikey. I took her pulse. "Take some nice deep breaths for me," I said. For once she obeyed.

Eventually her breathing became more regular. She looked me square in the eye, her face up close to mine. I braced myself for another set of sharp words.

"I knew I knew you," she said. "You're that nurse that looked after me at A&E." So! She really did remember me.

"You patched up the hand I slit cutting bread," she said. "You're too quiet! You need to talk to your patients more".

I remembered her then. I'd had to suture a nasty gash on her palm. I remembered thinking that no one would ever win an argument with this woman. "That's how you got so good with a needle," she told me, winked and grinned. My jaw dropped. It was so unexpected. "And you're a gaûchie," she said.

I looked at her helplessly. "A left-hander," translated Aurélie.

"Had to be a gaûchie to work in that corner. And you've got to be young and agile." Now, she was grinning broadly.

"You cheeky old Madam!" I gasped. Her eyes twinkled back at me naughtily.

I asked Aurélie later what Maman's real name was. "Cecily," she told me, "but she's Maman to everyone. As strong willed as they come! She had to be to bring up seven brothers during the Occupation on next to nothing. Everyone loves her to bits."

All those old photographs of the Occupation started to come to life for me that day. I started to understand what it was like for the independent minded Jersey people to be abandoned by the country they thought of as their Motherland, not Germany but England; for foreign occupiers to come in and rule them, frequently harshly; for families to be split apart, many never to return because of a cruel war. They must have had to face their fate with wills of iron.

I came to understand why the Liberation means so much to Jersey people. Listening as we worked to many more frightening, funny and often terribly, terribly sad stories from people who had lived through those difficult and uncertain days, endeared them to me permanently.

And, if ever there is another Occupation of Jersey and I get caught up in it, I would want to be with people just as strong and defiant as they can be.

MAY 1661, JERSEY

ANTHEA HALL

Anthea Hall Dip. I.G.A. is a fully qualified graphologist, (handwriting analyst) who now teaches the skill. She has written the History of Quakers in Jersey for the Société Jersiaise.

May 1661, Jersey – By Anthea Hall

Jeanne paused outside the study door, holding in one hand her ivory covered prayer book, her other hand poised to knock.

"Helier?"

Hearing the rustle of her silk petticoat, he opened the door and stood looking down upon her. All he could see was the top of her bent head covered by a woollen hood.

"Jeanne, come in. No need to knock, my dear."

"The carriage is waiting. Are you coming to church?" It was important to ask yet again knowing the answer would be no.

"You go. Take Cissy with you." He was anxious to return to his work.

"Helier?" she hesitated, "would you please dress well tonight. My parents will be at dinner, they like to see you in your velvet with the lace collar," she nearly added "...looking like the gentleman you are."

"To please you, yes. Now go or you will be late."

When she had gone he went back to the ledgers spread out upon the desk. The last few minutes had unsettled him. What was it about his wife, apart from her youth, that caused her to be so nervous, almost afraid of him? She, who could be so passionate in bed yet in the morning treating him with cool dignity and deferential formality. Certainly there was a large age gap between them, was that the whole answer? He knew he became irritated when he heard her laughing and giggling with her sisters, chattering about inconsequential matters between themselves then falling silent when he appeared. It troubled him knowing that she was sensitive to his moods. He didn't want to hurt her, his little butterfly of a wife with her pale eyes and soft silken hair that never lay flat, always escaping from her caps in boisterous tendrils.

He wished there could be a more natural relaxed relationship between them. If only he could talk to her freely, discuss his business ventures, the problems he encountered finding reliable crews for the ships he owned, plus keeping accurate accounts of the dickers of leather and tods of wool that made up the cargoes.

Sitting in her pew in the church of St Clement, Jeanne spent more time worrying than listening to the sermon. The church and its rituals had always been part of her life. She loved how the glittering candles lit up the murals now visible after being safely concealed and protected from the destructive actions of Cromwell's men, who, not so long ago smashed windows, destroying all objects of Catholic worship, breaking all there was to break.

Life in Jersey had resumed its pastoral ways now that Cromwell was dead and the King recalled from his enforced exile. The church, only partially restored, was still the haven of peace it always had been. Jeanne looked up at the mural of St Barbara who was pictured carrying a sheaf of corn in one hand, a sickle in the other, symbols of agriculture and summer, the tower where she had been imprisoned by her pagan father for her Christian beliefs painted in the background.

St Margaret, another female saint, emerging from the body of a dragon, was pictured on another wall. Jeanne, when a child, had nightmares about this mural until her nurse explained the story was symbolic of triumph over adversity, not mentioning the saint was the guardian of women in childbirth.

She remembered the happy occasions when she celebrated her first communion at the age of seventeen and her marriage to Helier a year later.

It had been flattering to be singled out for attention by an older man. A man who had travelled to many countries in the ships he owned, who had business dealings with her father, also called Helier. It was flattering to be looked upon with admiration. To be held in his gaze gave her an unaccustomed thrill of excitement of such pleasurable intensity she had lived with the feelings it gave for days afterwards. It was not a big surprise when he asked her father for her hand in marriage and no surprise that he readily agreed, pleased that one of his daughters at least would be a wealthy woman, and his farm, with the sheep he reared, secure for further transactions. Hastily kneeling and standing when required she went over and over the changes in Helier's behaviour which worried her during the past months ever since he had spent time in London.

She had always felt insignificant beside her educated and cultured husband. He spoke English well while she found difficulty with the language. She was conscious of being a farmer's daughter - educated at home while her brothers were sent to England for their schooling. His family were respected and treated as royalty in the Parish. She felt people looked down on her for being a country girl. Now it was humiliating as well, to sit in church without her husband by her side. Did he not realise how people would talk, how they would gossip about their relationship or lack of it?

It was also upsetting that he had not taken her to London. Before their marriage, Helier had met the young Prince of Wales when he first visited Jersey, and later, when the Island had proclaimed him King Charles the Second after the cruel death of his father, he made another visit and Helier was invited to functions at Elizabeth Castle where the royal party were staying.

Maybe in London another woman had captured Helier's fancy. Jeanne pictured a dark-haired beauty dressed in the latest fashion, conversing easily and intelligently about politics and current affairs. Her imagination quickly developed, carried by sparks of jealousy, until ashamed by her lurid fantasies she urgently recited, with the rest of the congregation, the creed, praying to be forgiven for her sins.

It was true that Helier had changed since he came back from his latest visit to England. He was happier, more relaxed, excited even, talking to the servants in a lighter voice, asking after their welfare and taking an interest in their lives which had never interested him before. He was kinder to the stable lads, none of whom had been beaten recently or punished for their idleness and boyish failings. This was unusual as was also the deliberate carelessness over dress. The new wig he had bought remained unworn; the embroidered suit and waist coats lay in the chest still in their wrappings.

The service ended, and with Cissy following, Jeanne made her way to the main door where the Rector was waiting to greet her. She made a slight bob of a curtsey to the old man.

"Ah Jeanne," he spoke in a low voice, not to be overheard. "How is Helier? I hope he is recovering from his cold."

She flushed at being reminded of the lies she had told to explain his absence.

The Rector went on. "You must love your husband, Jeanne, and always obey him."

His words hit her deep in her stomach as hard as a physical blow. Surely he did not believe she was a disobedient and uncaring wife? She who was always curbing her feelings, monitoring her every word not to give offence, careful never to criticise her husband over some of his actions, even if they disturbed her. It was often a struggle to be patient, to bear all things, to be pure and holy and of good intent. Surely she had succeeded? Obviously she had failed; otherwise the Rector would not have admonished her.

The small dinner party that night was a success. Helier was in great spirits regaling the company with amusing anecdotes how the English men could never pronounce his surname, Dumeresq, properly, and at Court, how Charles had teased him over the lack of partridges for the King's table, remembering the happy shooting parties he attended on the island. Helier did admit he was always glad to set sail for home away from the smells and dangers of disease in the big city of London.

85

The following morning, Jeanne was coming down the stairs when she was startled to see the front door opening and three rather disreputable men, still wearing their hats, walk straight into Helier's study without knocking or any servant announcing them. She had seen two of the men before, probably business clients from a different Parish; the third man was a stranger, a foreigner by the look of him. They had not arrived on horses, as their boots were muddy.

Jeanne expected Helier to eject them immediately but as time went past, as she stood waiting on the stairs, nothing happened. She became more and more concerned when they did not appear, and wondered if she ought to call a servant. Creeping down the stairs lifting her skirts not to make a sound, she put her ear to the door and listened, hoping to hear what was said. She heard nothing. There was silence from the room. Time passed. Her back began to ache, so, still trembling and frightened, she moved to the drawing room where she sat until over an hour later the men left quickly and without ceremony.

Immediately, she challenged Helier at the open door of the study, noting he was rearranging the chairs. Had the men been invited to sit?

"Who were those men? What did they want? Are you in trouble Helier? Were they asking for money? You must tell me, I am so frightened." The words came out in a rush.

He took both her hands in his and gently led her to a chair. Sitting opposite her, he said quietly, "Jeanne, I am so sorry you are upset. I have been meaning to tell you something for a long time but hadn't the courage." He lowered his eyes looking at her hands which still lay in his.

86

"Another woman?" she faltered.

He smiled. "No, no my love." He was about to laugh. "I am a Quaker."

"A Quaker!" She pulled her hands away and stood up. "You are a Quaker, a heretic? It's not possible."

"Jeanne, please listen, I will explain. I will tell you what the seekers of truth believe. Nothing sinister, I assure you."

She sank back into her chair, shocked and confused but stilled by the intensity of his voice, his eyes shining and bright, as he told her how Quakers sit in silence believing they are led by the prompting of the spirit which lay in everyone.

It was not in praying and singing, not in doctrines, nor images or crosses or the sprinkling of infants, but in the realities of life. Jesus Christ and the love of God was everywhere at all times, not just in the churches, he told her. All people were equal and women were called upon to speak at meetings, not just the men.

"We are people," he went on to say, "that follow after these things that make for peace, love and unity; it is our desire that others' feet may walk in the same, and we do deny and bear our testimony against all strife and wars and contentions."

It wasn't easy. It took a while for Jeanne to understand and accept this new philosophy. This was just the beginning of a new chapter in their marriage. She was encouraged to speak freely, to argue with passion with Helier over many subjects.

She discovered she was adept with numbers, enabling her to keep accounts of all the shipping cargoes.

Men were soon lining up to crew the ships knowing that their families would be looked after when they were away at sea. Flogging was forbidden. The food would be plentiful and the pay fair and promptly paid.

Jeanne was encouraged to speak freely, to argue with passion with Helier over many subjects. All because Quakers, the Religious Society of Friends, had come into their lives.

Helier became a pioneer of the Cod Fishing Industry sailing to the Gaspé peninsular in Newfoundland. He would never have guessed that three hundred years later his ships would be featured in the Maritime Museum, New North Quay, St Helier.

HELERIUS UNMASKED

ROY MCCARTHY

Roy McCarthy is a Finance Manager by day and a keen runner and athletics coach. He has self-published four books including two historical novels set in Jersey.

Helerius Unmasked – By Roy McCarthy

"How now, good morning Jacob, old friend."

"Good morning Helerius, are you well?"

"Very well, yes. Do you bring news from the town?"

"I do. But I bring more. Here."

"Ah! Bread, apples. Thank you old friend. So, what news? How is the Widow Maud?"

"She is brighter. She sends her thanks and says that when she is fully better, she will come and visit with a little food and whatever else she can spare."

"Pshaw! Food perhaps, but I have no need for anything else. What other news?"

"The girl-child is healthy. But the old man grows weaker. Will you visit him Helerius?"

"Yes, I will visit. Tomorrow. It won't stop nature taking its course but it might bring a little comfort."

The two men sat atop a grassy rock surveying the land and sea. To their right the long, sandy beach and the poor settlement in the dunes that served as the town of the island of Gersi. There were other small villages and hamlets scattered about the wild island but most travellers that came and stayed set up home here on the coast among the low dunes.

Over to the west a harbour and another modest settlement, and it was from here that several small wooden fishing vessels plied the local waters, their nets trailing, making the most of the fine weather. Once the winter storms set in, the people had to live on what they had put aside in the autumn. Fish and meat preserved in salt, grain for bread-making, little else.

But today was fine. The clouds were high, a light breeze blew from the south and life was easier for the islanders. Some of the people could be seen from where the two men gazed, moving between the poor dwellings, walking to and from the higher slopes where animals were tended and crops grew.

"Helerius, do you ever wonder about your former life in Gaul? Your parents, friends, your mentor?"

"No I do not. Why do you ask?"

"You were not sorry to leave them when you were sent here?"

"Sorry? My friend Jacob, it was a happy day that I left them to live here in Gersi. There I had to work hard. Here I can sit and watch the sea and sky and do no work."

"But Helerius, you do much work and it is good. You teach the people Christian ways. You have the power to heal, to make the people happy. They bless the ground you walk on and bow as you approach. Does this not please you?"

Helerius threw back his head and laughed merrily, but offered no answer. He scratched his beard, threw a pebble at a rock, said nothing. Jacob went on,

"Before the winter storms and cold arrive will you come to live with us in the town, Helerius? We will build the best of dwellings for you. You will be comfortable and warm. Plenty of food. Maybe you will take a wife?" Helerius's eyes twinkled, his beard twitched and he shook his head firmly. Jacob continued. "I understand. You are a hermit. It is your calling to live alone, without comforts, so that you can commune with your God, give yourself to him alone. But you can perform your good works even better if you are comfortable and strong. The people will care for you."

Helerius turned to Jacob and answered, "I am happy here on the islet and I have my cave for when the winds blow and the rain and sleet sweep through."

"I see. You deny yourself comforts the better to perform your good works."

Helerius sighed. "My friend, I don't think you are listening. I am not denying myself anything. I don't want to live in the town. I prefer it here."

"I see, because..."

"Because nothing! Because I like it here!"

"But we can offer you proper shelter."

"I have shelter, there in my cave which never leaks or blows down. Your huts leak and blow down in the winter gales and you need to mend them. I have the nicest place."

"But it is cold, you have no fire."

"I have plenty of furs which you people insist on giving to me. I am never cold. From what I see all the people of the town are wet and miserable in winter. I am not."

"We share our food among us when times get hard…"

"You and the others bring me food! Sometimes I have too much and throw it to the gulls while your children cry with hunger."

They sat in silence. In a while the causeway would be covered by the encroaching tide and Jacob would need to leave to cross safely back to the dunes. But he found Helerius uncommonly talkative today. Some days he would say little or nothing. Jacob pressed on.

"Are there not times when you desire companionship? People to talk to?"

"There are not. What do I want to talk about? Why do I wish to take a wife to have to listen to her babbling the day and night long with babies mewling and crying? In your town the men talk nonsense over their ale and fall to fighting. Here on my rock I need be bothered by no one. I like my own company."

"You are a good and holy man, Helerius."

"I am not holy." Helerius said. "The Christianity I preach I have no faith in. It is mumbo jumbo, no more or less than those that still worship the ancient pagan gods. But if it gives the people comfort and common cause then I am happy to continue to preach. Just don't ask me to believe any of it."

Jacob laughed. "Helerius, this is a good joke. Tell me then, how do you perform your miracles if your true God does not exist?"

"Ah Jacob, this is an easy trick. If a cripple walks again it is because of his inner faith, not because of my doing. If he does not walk then it is thought to be God's will. If a sick child dies it is nature's way. If it recovers then I have performed a miracle. The potions I administer may work or they may not. If they do I take the credit. If they do not then I take no blame. I always win. There, does this surprise you?"

"Helerius, you are a funny man. You are pulling my leg. If you were truly a false hermit then you would not speak in such a way. The people would cease to listen to you and would not worship your God."

"So Jacob, maybe you begin to understand. Yes I wish to continue with this fine, lazy life with the people of the town catering for my every need. Of course I will sit here on a rock and let you all think I am a bringer of miracles from the one true God. I can think of no finer occupation."

"Helerius, I am happy to find you in such jovial spirits, to hear you jest about these gifts that you bring to us. You truly are God's servant."

94

And as Jacob hurried back across the causeway to wife, children, village and work, Helerius sighed and lay back on his rock. Snuggled up in a fur, enjoying the last rays of the sun from over the cliffs to the west, he watched as three Viking ships rounded the southern rocks, picked up pace, and headed for the bay.

GHOSTLY ENCOUNTERS

ELIZABETH LAWRENCE

Elizabeth is a writer and Poet. She has received awards for her Short Stories and Poetry. She enjoys all aspects of writing and is currently working on her first novel.

Ghostly Encounters (with a fair bit of mayhem thrown in) – By Elizabeth Lawrence

The Family's surname was Darling, and much to Ambrose's annoyance, his wife Prue used it as an affectionate form of address; she really should have known better, for as a child his name had made him the butt of many a joke. His irritation was compounded when an American couple moved into the village, and, on being introduced to Prue and Ambrose, were heard to say later, "well aren't they just darling."

Prue sat at the breakfast table and flicked through the pages of her latest recipe book, "Darling, why don't I cook us something special for dinner?"

"Can't do old thing, I have a meeting this evening." He noticed the crestfallen look upon her face and felt a twinge of guilt followed swiftly by an anticipatory whiff of perfumed promise at the thought of the night ahead.

At the front door she received a dry peck on the cheek. What, she asked herself, had happened to the passion in their marriage, she watched him haul himself into his car, he'd grown a little portly of late: she took a perverse pleasure in this observation and closed the door.

She was delighted when, a little later, her daughter Kate rang inviting her to join the family on an organised Moonlight Walk commencing in Gorey.

"Julian's the Ghost host; it should be great fun; ghouls, ghosts and spine-tingling stories. He says to wrap up warmly, wear sensible shoes and bring a torch."

Prue smiled, "Very Green Room your friend Julian, he'll be in his element."

"Don't be mean Mummy; we'll pick you up just after 9.30pm."

"Isn't that a little late for Meg to be out darling?" A picture of her granddaughter came into her mind, a precocious, high-spirited child, with Harry Potter glasses, two long, skinny plaits and last, but not least, a sweet smile camouflaged by metal braces. "Forget I said that, Meg has more staying power than I'll ever have."

As instructed by Julian they gathered with the rest of the group in Gorey Village. In the disappearing twilight, Mont Orgueil Castle loomed overhead; it was going to be a perfect night for monsters and mayhem. Eventually a tall figure minced towards them, donning a top hat, scarlet cravat, a black cape and, held in his gloved fingers, an ebony cane: with a haughty stare he watched as two buxom ladies walked towards him.

"'Scuse me love," one of them said, peering at his nameplate, "Perigrine is it? Are we with you?" With a theatrical flourish he checked his pocket-watch, frowned and with an audible sigh said "You're a touch tardy – ladies."

"What's that mean?"

Meg, who was standing nearby said "You're a bit late." She turned her attention to the tall figure.

"Uncle Julian, Granny says you look pompous."

Julian's eyes narrowed as he looked towards Prue, who on seeing him waved enthusiastically.

Meg continued, "and camp," she shrugged her shoulders, "whatever that means," and fingering the silky, red lining of his cape she gazed up at him "but I think you look - magnificent!"

"Why thank you Meg, now please leave my cape alone."

He turned to the assembled group, "I trust you are all suitably attired," there was a murmuring of assent. "Then follow me."

They walked up the steep incline behind the buildings to the castle and gathered around Julian. The night was living up to its billing; the moonlight cast ominous shadows in an otherwise still, starlit sky. Clearing his throat, Julian, his voice sepulchral in tone, proceeded to address the group.

"May I suggest that if any of you are of a nervous disposition it might be advisable to leave now, for the journey we are about to undertake will be fraught with..." he felt a slight tug and looking down saw Meg examining his cape. Through clenched teeth he hissed, "If you don't stop playing with that..." then, realizing the group were waiting, he continued, eyes fixed on Meg. "Terror."

Prue dismissed Julian with an icy stare, "C'mon Meg, take Granny's hand and..."

At that precise moment an indistinct shape arose on the castle green, an old woman dressed in white, hands outstretched, began to moan and keen.

"Ouch! Granny you're hurting me," Meg said prising her hand from Prue's grasp.

"Sorry darling, didn't you find that scary?" she received a long-suffering look.

"Anyway," she continued, "what's this I hear, Mummy said you'd lost your laugh - how awful."

"Yes, it's quite worrying, Granny."

"You mean it hasn't come back yet?"

Meg sighed, "No, not really, it's just a little tee hee hee and then it goes again."

Prue and Meg caught up with the others; Julian was relating a tale about a huge, rampaging bull that could be heard along the coast at low tide. Meg felt a tug on her pigtails, she turned and glowered, a scruffy boy dressed in a loin cloth and tattered leather shirt stood just behind her, "Do that again," she threatened, and so he did. Meg gave him one of her special smiles. "You are silly, I didn't mean for you to actually do it - duh." she stared at him, "What's your name and aren't you a bit cold dressed like that?" The boy just shrugged. "Hmm. I think I'll call you Fred."

"Meg darling, do stop talking to yourself, you know what they..."

"Granny, I'm not! I'm talk..." Meg's eyes widened, she turned again to the boy, "Are you a ghost?"

He grinned and nodded his head. "That's just -," Meg thought for a moment, "stupendous! - Granny!" her shout was met with some disapproval, especially from Julian, who was in full flow.

"And in 1551, all the church bells in Jersey were removed and shipped to France, but the vessel carrying them sank shortly after departure. It is now said that anyone who hears the bells while at sea," at this point the sound of distant bells could be heard offshore, "will not make it back to land."

Louis, a fisherman of little renown, had dropped anchor and whilst reading a 'magazine' had dozed off, as is often the case in old age. Dreaming of nubile mermaids, his delightful reverie came to an abrupt end at the sound of the bells, he stood up with some difficulty and gasped "Mon Dieu! The bells! The bells!"

Unaware of Louis's existence below them and his dilemma with boat and balance, the group moved on.

Meg smiled at her new companion, "I'm so pleased I've met you Fred, 'cause this evening is all a bit boring except for you that is, and even you're not very scary."

The boy appeared to think about this and then, tapping his finger on the side of his nose, she watched him disappear up the long incline towards the houses at the top where Uncle Julian lived.

Julian was now relating a story about a large, black dog called Le Tchan de Bouole, sometimes seen dragging a heavy chain. At that moment there was a rustling in the nearby hedge and something that sounded like a metal chain. A few nervous giggles ensued, but these turned to terrified screams as a large, black dog hurtled towards them from the top of the lane.

As the dog drew nearer, Julian realized it was Norman, his Russian Terrier, who looked more like a bear than a dog. Julian was trying to figure out how he'd escaped when Norman hurled himself at his owner, lavishing him with wet kisses as he felled him.

Julian, always ready to take centre stage, decided to use this incident to his advantage, and started to flail his arms and kick his legs, accompanied by the appropriate groans and shouted "Get this evil beast off me!"

Meg burst out laughing, "Stop pretending, Uncle Julian, you know it's only Norman." Julian gave her a withering look which she ignored.

"Why darling, you've found your laugh!" Prue said, and then noticed that Julian's dog was lying on its back with its legs in the air, "Meg, is something wrong with Norman?"

Meg watched the boy rubbing Norman's tummy, then turned towards Prue, "Possibly a touch of colic, Granny," and whispered to Fred, "You let Norman out, didn't you?" he nodded. "Awesome!" she said.

Julian, dusted himself down and with Norman slavering by his side, continued, "Quite soon we will reach Victoria Tower, the last Martello tower to be built."

The group, still a little shaken, followed him to the top of the lane.

The small car park adjacent to the Tower was a favourite parking place for lovers, as it overlooked the beautiful bay of Anne Port, Mont Orgueil Castle and St Catherine's Breakwater. Ambrose was surprised but delighted that his was the only car parked here. He turned towards his companion to embrace her, "You really are a fine filly, Olga."

"My name is not Olga, its Helga."

For an instant Ambrose had a vision of his granddaughter Meg, shrugging her shoulders and saying "Whatever."

"I'm so sorry my sweet one, now where were we, ah yes..." he showered her with kisses, "Oh Olga, Olga," he moaned.

"It's Helga! Helga!"

Ambrose chose to ignore the stridency of her tone and was about to suggest they move to the back seat for comfort. It was at this point that they became aware of shadowy figures approaching them, accompanied by random, ethereal spots of bobbing lights.

"Oh mein Gott! They are ghosts yes?"

Julian thought the car looked familiar, a couple of the group decided to investigate further and shone their torches into the

103

steamed up windows, making a few ribald comments as they did so. Just as the enormity of the situation dawned on him he heard Meg say, in a matter of fact voice "That's Grandad's car." Then waving her arms as if in a greeting ran on towards the Dolmen and her friend.

Julian felt the panic rise in his craw, where was Kate and her ghastly mother! It was with some relief to see that they had walked ahead towards the Tower, deep in conversation, oblivious to the parked car. Julian, with mounting hysteria summoned the group to him, and after completing a hasty, potted history, led them away from the Tower towards the Faldouet Dolmen.

Meg watched with delight and clapped her hands as Fred danced a jig on the capstone, whilst in the background a man, dressed in a similar way to Fred, shook his head smiling and beckoned the boy to his side. The boy looked at the man and then at Meg, he walked towards her, she felt a soft, icy sensation upon her cheek then Fred was gone.

"Meg! Will you please hurry up," her mother shouted, "everyone's waiting for you."

As they neared Mont Orgueil Castle they heard the continuous sound of a car horn, as if something or someone was jammed up against it, this was followed by a piercing scream.

The sound seemed to originate from the top of the hill close to Victoria Tower. The group turned as one towards the commotion. Julian paled visibly and watched with dread as Prue approached him. He decided there and then that he'd had enough of this malarkey and would hand in his resignation post-haste.

Prue, unaware of his deathly pallor, linked her arm through his.

"Hats off to you Julian! What a delicious, satisfying end to the evening."

LIBERATED

JON STASIAK

Jon Stasiak graduated with a degree in Fine Art. In addition to painting and his photography, Jon has self-published a number of short stories available for Kindle. He is currently putting the finishing touches to his first novel, *Standing in the Shadows*.

Liberated – By Jon Stasiak

To my beloved sons,

I fear this will be the last chance I have to be honest with you. I wish to detail my side of the story and to explain exactly what happened to our family back when you were young boys growing up in Jersey. Please remember that I always intended to protect you both: to shield you from the wicked hand of your father. I desperately wished for you to be brought up in a happy, healthy environment without fear; a life I could not afford myself. I dearly hope that most of this letter will come as a shock to you, as I must believe any of what you had witnessed has long since been repressed. My intent is not to try and taint your own memories of your father; who I know loved you in his own way, but to give truth to the circumstances of why you were to grow up without him.

However, if, after reading on, you still wish to hold my actions against me, then I will go to my grave with the comfort of honesty, and at least on my part, as clear a conscience as I might deserve. I remember the below as if it was yesterday.

Here we go again, I feared, not for the first time that week. I had suffered at the violent hands of your father for as long as I could remember, and this occasion seemed to be no different.

Your father and I had met when we were very young and we knew nothing of a life without one other. We married in our teens, and after the untimely loss of both my parents, before you, I had no one to call family but him. The emotional abuse began early. He oppressed me and verbally dominated me on a daily basis for several years before the beatings began.

After bearing him two children, three bouts in hospital and four years of violent misery, I had almost got used to a life of submissive servitude. The only light at the end of my very dark tunnel, being you, my two dearly loved sons.

"Can't you get anything right, woman?" He shouted violently… "You know I don't like it this way!"

I could feel his hot, beer-tempered breath as he spat his words in my face. This time, apparently, his potatoes were overdone and his coffee too cold. Once again, I hadn't served his dinner quite as he liked it after returning from an afternoon of drinking in the pub. I would be punished severely for the mistake.

I silently sighed and prepared to take the worst of it. My arms were still bruised from the last time he hit me, but then, it was much better to protect my face. After all, I was always able to hide my wounded arms from you. Another black eye or broken jaw would have been much harder to conceal, and I couldn't bear leaving you in favour of a hospital bed for the night.

"I've put up with your food for far too long…" He went on, raising his hand to me.

"Enough!" I snapped back, completely out of character.

I don't know what had come over me. Never before had I even dared to look him in the eye during one of his tempers. However, this time, the words I never had the courage to speak escaped me before I could contain them.

Taken aback by my abruptness, his frozen glare of surprise offered me just enough time to escape the confines of the kitchen. I quickly ran for the door, slamming it behind me before he could even call out my name.

Leaving our beloved cottage behind on that summer's evening, I ran out towards Archirondel, my favourite place on the island. I was desperate to protect you from witnessing one of my beatings and would hide you at any cost. Quickly, I grabbed your little hands as you played out on the grass and we ran as swiftly as we could towards the red and white tower in search of shelter.

Your father and I had spent all of our married life together in that little fisherman's cottage near Havre de Fer. I had twice given birth in that very house and even with the terrible memories I had of him in there, I still fondly called it home. The thought of leaving your father; my wicked husband, had crossed my mind many times since the violence began. But, what could I do with two little boys to take care of? Where would we go?

We had no other family. Nowhere else to turn. I knew of no other refuge back then that would protect us. Unfortunately, this was the life that I had been assigned. Brunt and bear it, I told myself. As long as I could shield you from the violence, as long as he never laid a finger on either of you, I hoped that one day, things would eventually turn out ok. I might have been a broken woman, but at least I had my little home and my beautiful boys to show for it, I reasoned.

Panicked, I was fearful of what he might do when he caught me. Never before had I argued back, let alone run away from him. I was scared of the consequences. Thinking of you out there with me, I instantly wished I had taken the beating quietly, behind closed doors, rather than subjecting you to it. I was fearful, yet also strangely excited at my first act of liberation.

As we made our way past the closed café, I desperately hoped he wasn't following us. I only wanted a little bit of space, a few hours away from him, in the company of my boys.

Hopefully, by then he'd have had enough time to calm down. Better still, I wished that he might be drunk enough to have forgotten all about it.

"Get back here!" I heard from somewhere behind.

The words cut through me like glass. Looking down, your unknowing, fearful faces broke my heart. Keeping quiet, we made it to the tower. I didn't know if had he seen us, or was just shouting aimlessly.

"I won't tell you again." He slurred.

Covering your little ears from his taunts, I whispered for you to hide in the long grass. I urged you to keep quiet and promised you lots of kisses on winning the game of 'hide and seek' with your father. Never in my life had I been as fearful as when I left you in the grass to confront him.

"Enough!" I screamed, not knowing what I was to do.

Stood below me, he'd made his way down to the rocky beach on which the tower had been built.

"Get down here!" He demanded as he swayed from either the alcohol he'd consumed, or the uneven terrain underfoot.

"No. Leave me. Please leave me be." I begged.

But I knew then that it was too late to go back. To pretend, as I had done for years, that his beating didn't happen. Every time before, each attack had gone without reaction. I had never complained, I had never argued and I had never spoken of them afterwards. I was too afraid. However now that I'd escaped him, now that I had broken free from his hand, I just knew I couldn't ignore the abuse anymore. I knew he wouldn't let me. If I was to survive the beating that was waiting for me below, I'd never have been able to hide it from you as I had done in the past.

Scrambling over the damp, loose rock of low tide, your father made his way around the base of Archirondel for me. I begged him to stop. I begged and begged him to leave me be, to let me take my children and be free of him, but he wouldn't let me. I was his possession, as were you, and it was his prerogative to deal with me, with us, as he saw fit.

I could see the anger in his eyes as he made his way up the steps to apprehend me. My fearful screaming only angered him more. Not only was he promising to teach me a lesson, but this time he promised to take his anger out on the two of you. He told me that any action taken out on you both was as a result of my insubordination and lack of respect. The thought of him beating you because I escaped him was too much for my heart to bear. I snapped.

As a vulnerable woman in charge of two young boys, in that split moment, I lost my sense of reason. Frightened for my life, and the protection of my children I did what any good mother would do.

Reaching down to the granite underfoot, I frantically dug for a loose piece of brickwork, a boulder or rock big enough to protect me.

Then he approached me. I thought it was too late. Grabbing my wrist, he threw me to the ground. I will never forget the sting of pain as my head cracked against the sharp, unforgiving granite.

As if that torture wasn't enough, he towered over me, slapping and punching me. It was enough for me to want to close my eyes and go to sleep forever more. I slowly rolled my head, trying to protect what I could of my face, and then I saw it. Enough to make me protect myself and fight back. Stood in the long grass, not too far from where I was getting beaten to death, I saw you both. Transfixed in fear, the look on both of your faces gave me the power to save myself, for your sake, if not my own.

Grasping outwards, whilst he continued to assault me from above I managed to scratch around and dislodge a sizable chunk of heavy rock. Your father, so arrogant in his ability to dominate me, didn't expect me to fight back. He didn't consider that I might have reason enough to want to protect you both. He didn't expect me to crack him around the head with a deadening blow from behind. With it, I'd managed to knock him off me. As he lay to one side, I brought the granite down again and again on his skull until I knew the job was done and I, we were free.

I wiped my own blood-soaked hair from my brow as I collapsed on top of him from pure exhaustion.

I woke up to the warmth of your embrace. I remember vividly, both of you warning me to get up before 'daddy' woke up and hit me again. It was then I knew I'd finally done right by you both. I told you to let yourself back into the house whilst I tidied up and took care of 'daddy'.

Fortunately, the police didn't even question your father's death the next day, when he washed up on the pebbly shore. It seems that the 'local drunk' living next to the granite beach of Harve de Fer had been an accident waiting to happen for some time. Your father's head wound was consistent with him taking an intoxicated fall from the tower onto the unforgiving stone below. The strong tide battered his body further into the jagged rocks, and satisfied the coroner's final report.

As I lay here on my own death bed, a new woman after liberating myself from a wrecked marriage, I hope you can forgive me. I hope you can look back over repressed memories and forgive me from not liberating myself much earlier.

I love you both and hope you can one day enjoy the beautiful island of Jersey the way I had before I met your father.

WHEN THE TIDE TURNS

KAREN FORBES

Karen has been an English/ Drama teacher for 30+ years and was formerly a freelance journalist/ editor for a local publisher in East Anglia. She has a particular interest in theatre directing, and script writing for the screen and stage.

When the Tide Turns – By Karen Forbes

A canoe, bruised hull, splintered and upturned, bobs gently amidst the spangled dark-turquoise bay, the perils of a subsiding riptide disguised, forgotten beneath the mirrored surface. Far out across St. Catherine's Bay, the distant Condor ferry heads for St-Malo churning off-white foam in her wake, eagerly making up time lost by fog earlier in the day. A lone cormorant dips its bill in search of mackerel, flips upside down, and vanishes from sight into the undertow.

He couldn't remember when he had stopped listening, he simply had. There seemed very little left in his world worth listening to and he certainly didn't want to be drawn into idle chit-chat, particularly this evening. Barry Browne, reserved and inconspicuous in his grey parka, rucksack bulging between his feet, sits in the same seat, at the same time (give or take an hour, depending on the tides), with the same people, every Friday evening. They are commuters making their weekly voyage from France to St. Helier Harbour. Jersey weekenders, laden with French cigarettes, fortified wines and carefully wrapped wedges of Brie and Camembert, homeward bound to their loved ones after a week away, working in the provinces. Every Monday morning, except for school vacations, Bank holidays and Liberation Day, Barry reluctantly joins them for the return trip, his suitcase replete with laundered clothes, travel-size toiletries and piles of carefully annotated essays awaiting return to his latest class of foreign language students.

115

Forty-seven (forty-eight this weekend he corrects himself) is too old for anyone to keep this lark up, he grumbles behind his newspaper. Up and down the length of the cabin deck a Portuguese steward scoops paper coffee cups and sticky cellophane sandwich cartons into a black refuse sack as though he could do it blindfolded. The regulars seem oblivious to the litter they have discarded, preferring to jostle for position in the queue for the duty free shop, or the queue for the toilets, or the queue for the over-priced cafeteria. Predictably, he observes, they will even queue for the car deck and the foot-passenger exit signs, long before the vessel has docked at the Jersey quayside. They are noisy, raucous even, with their beer-tinged breath and bargain-bin aftershave. Today, he decides, he has had enough.

In a secluded corner seat, on the top deck of the bus travelling from Liberation Square to Gorey, glimpsing other people's swimming pools, roof-top gardens and ornamental rose bushes in ceramic tubs, Barry feels more subdued than usual. Not because his week has been more taxing than usual. Not because he is concerned that the recent spate of redundancies at his French language school will impinge on him, particularly. It is simply the fact that he is bored. Bored and weary of his monotonous routine. His presence this weekend, in fact most weekends, will hardly be noticed amidst the endless round of domestic chores Geraldine will have lined up for him. Leaves in the pool, configuring a new router for the internet, a damaged light in the garage, the weekly Waitrose grocery run (complete with own brand birthday slab and blue candles)...

He was finding it difficult to remember the last time they had been out together, just the two of them, walking their dog Rory on the white sands of St. Ouen or ordering a meal for two at their local, The Dolphin. Barry missed Maddy and Peter, recently escaped to university overseas and leading lives of their own, most of all. Although he hated their mess, now the house felt unlived in, too neat, too tidy, echoes replacing teenage banter. Occasionally, he would Facetime them over a weekend, but more often than not the timing was wrong: they were either on their way to sample cheap beer at the student bar, or it was Sunday lunchtime and neither of them had surfaced from their campus duvets yet.

The bus pulls out of Liberation Square and turns left onto the coast road. Barry wistfully recollects the occasions, at low tide, when he has walked them out to Elizabeth Castle, small hands gripping his, excitedly debating whether they would get back before the tide turned or end up stranded inside the castle, alongside the ghosts of forgotten soldiers and Sir Walter Raleigh. This was always their excuse to use the Puddle Ducks, wonderfully inventive motorised contraptions which turned into floating bath tubs as the waters rose around you and carried you safely back to the shore. This Friday evening, as the sun settles lower on the horizon and the castle fades from view, Barry realises he has forgotten to pick up the dry cleaning on his way home and that the Puddle Ducks are no longer waiting beside the tourist office to chauffeur passers-by.

Gemini Cottage, located on the main road leading to Gorey Pier, overlooks Mont Orgueil, a spectacular castle, formerly the residence of the Governors of Jersey; more recently, an impressive setting for modern weddings and one of the most photographed locations in Jersey, famed for its panoramic views. Barry could have written the guidebook himself. Every time he glimpses a bridal entourage wending their way cautiously to the top of the medieval turrets, flip-flop clad, satin stilettos in hand, he recalls the days of his own wedding in the village church. Not quite so grand, but grand enough to make him relieved when his father-in-law puts his hand in his pocket and he realises he isn't footing the bill alone.

Geraldine had been enchanted from the moment she set eyes on the house. Not only did she love the high tech kitchen and sprawling lounge, she also loved the name. "Gemini...twins...split personality," she whispered mischievously, winking in Barry's direction. The estate agent sensed victory. Hastily, he ushered the bride-to-be through the French windows onto the equally impressive balcony, two storeys up, to get a better look. In that moment, Geraldine drank in the breath-taking views, the idyllic mesh of rhythmical fishing boats laced together in the harbour, the Ecréhous isles stretching across the horizon, and the deal was clinched. There was no denying the views were magnificent, unspoiled by architectural intervention and naturally beautiful. "After all," she cooed, "we can splash out a bit since my parents are putting up the deposit." It was impossible to say no, especially as Mr Cornish senior had made such strong overtures about his future son-in-law joining the family business one day, once he was retired. "Anyway, how many people can say they live almost opposite a family monument?" Geraldine boasted. And he was reminded, not for the first time, of her intention to retain her maiden name once they were married.

Sure enough, as if on cue, one crisp autumn morning two years after moving in, Geraldine gave birth to twins, a boy and a girl, the perfect pair. "Job done," she joked with her coffee-

118

morning girlfriends, more serious than they had realised, "...just in time to meet my 'end of year' deadline." And so Barry's wife slipped almost seamlessly back into her fast-track career at the bank, securing a hefty, end-of-year bonus into the bargain, never to return to domesticity, as they knew it, ever again. Her colleagues barely had time to notice she hadn't been there.

Organising and planning are Geraldine's forte; they always have been. From booking the Caesarian section birth and hiring the nanny, to walking the dog and booking bargain flights online, Geraldine has become a grand master of time-management; cramming as much into their already overflowing lives as possible. "Living life to the full," she calls it, "you never know what's around the corner." It has become her regular Saturday morning mantra. She is showering in the en-suite bathroom, after her run. "You should take up a hobby, if you're bored. Get fit. Check out sailing or canoeing, or something. There's always the Hotel de France gym. Pass me the towel will you, please."

Barry reaches for the white fluffy bath towel above the 'his and hers' granite-veined sinks. They had been all the rage four years ago. Of course it was the most expensive display model in the showroom, but the young salesman - sharp-suited and keener than mustard - offered a further discount on the sale price, clinching the deal with a new monthly installment scheme for first time customers. It was a no-brainer. Barry didn't even attempt resistance, dutifully signing on the dotted line whilst Geraldine waltzed into the adjacent furnishings section in search of matching blinds and appliances.

Yes, spending money and saving time were certainly her priorities these days. She even booked his vasectomy during the half-term break so that neither of them would have to waste precious days from their annual leave entitlement. And so they settled into a life beyond babies, nurseries, parent evenings and A' levels, each event hastily replaced by another; returning to the weekend dinner party circuit which Geraldine had been so very fond of. It was a far cry from their university days where she had persuaded him to follow her to the island to be nearer to her family. It was costing money, he worried, escalating by the year. So when a chance promotion at the language school in Guemene-sur-Scorff arose, she deemed this the perfect solution, especially since they were facing university fees in duplicate.

Barry unfolds his copy of L'Express and sips the freshly ground Lavazza lovingly placed beside him. Alongside, a slice of syrup-drenched Opera cake, homemade, no candles - his favourite. It is Sunday; the morning of his fiftieth birthday. He muses at the imaginary headlines in the Jersey Evening Post and wonders how long it will be before somebody notices that his regular seat on the ferry is empty. He glances at the pile of euro coins, small change from the corner shop in Guemene and smiles contentedly. Not quite the treasure haul metal-detector enthusiasts have recently unearthed from a nearby field in Grouville, but he has enough.

Money hardly matters to him these days. Geraldine can have all the money she has ever dreamed of, once the life insurance company settles her claim. He's not the first and he won't be the last. A gentle hand rests warmly on his shoulder. The same hand which furnished him with lavishly garnished petit fours and slices of rich Tarte Tatin a year ago now wears

120

his wedding ring. A chance meeting across a stall at a French Christmas market in Royal Square. He orders in French; Veronique remembers the name of his house as she records the post code. He is charmed by her dark eyes and beautiful smile. On her French lips, "Gemini" sounds like melting chocolate.

Nowadays, he dreams of wealth immeasurable; but wealth of a very different kind from the one he has left behind.

A Knock at the Door

Marianne Le Boutillier

Marianne Le Boutillier was born and raised in Jersey and trained as primary school teacher. She is the author of *The King Behind the Picture*, and, as well as other stories, has written lyrics for two short musicals.

A Knock at the Door – By Marianne Le Boutillier

A knock on the door cut through the comforting sound of the crackling fire and she pushed her huge ginger cat off her lap, annoyed that she would lose her warm, live cushion. Opening the door, she peered into the fading light.

"Yes?" she said, a question resonating both irritation and curiosity.

"Good evening. Um, Mrs Forster isn't it?" replied a tall, smart, very young man. "I'm here about the damp."

"The damp," she repeated.

"Yes, we're doing a great deal of work in this area and your wonderful old property is typical of the homes we've been working on. These granite houses are such a problem, aren't they, Mrs Forster? We know that damp-proofing can help protect you against the onset of rising damp and mildew. We can sort out the ventilation too and finish our work with damp seal paint, of course."

"Oh!" she said. Precocious lad, she thought.

"It's mighty cold out here, could we possibly discuss it inside?" he asked, stamping his feet and rubbing his hands together. He smiled, a smile that infuriated her, but she stood aside and gestured for him to enter.

"Tea?" she asked.

"Cool! Milk and two sugars please."

He studied Mrs Forster as she reached the open kitchen door and turned, looking at him through her thick horn-rimmed glasses. Then she pushed a lock of tightly permed white hair back into place and disappeared from sight. He grinned. This was going to be easy. She'd be signing on the dotted line and his commission would pay for a round of beers at the pub before the night had even begun.

He scanned the room as he heard the clatter of kettle and tea cups in the kitchen. It looked as if nothing had changed for years. Just an old threadbare sofa, a dark mahogany bookcase and coffee table, an armchair with a crochet blanket slung over its back and an ancient ginger cat. At each end of the mantelpiece was a small blue vase, one filled with snowdrops and the other with dried flowers, and a clock ticked contentedly next to a picture of a young man in a 1940's army uniform.

"Please sit," she invited, as she returned with the tea, put it on the table and sat in her chair. "Yours is in the green cup."

In the silence, only interrupted by the popping fir cones on the fire and slurping of tea, he felt distinctly uncomfortable. He shuffled in his seat and cleared his throat.

"Well, Mrs Forster, what a lovely home you have."

"Yes, isn't it," she replied, with a slight nod of her head.

"But these old granite houses are very cold, don't you think? Rising damp's a big problem. Not good for the lungs, Mrs Forster. Or rheumatism," he added as an afterthought. "Damp-proofing will help protect you against the onset of rising damp and mildew. We can sort out the ventilation too and finish our work with damp seal paint, of course."

"Did you learn that from a book?" she asked quietly.

Ignoring her, he hurried on with the next part of his sales pitch. "And Radon gas too, Mrs Forster. This could be a very dangerous house with gas seeping out of the granite walls. Also bad for the lungs. A very frightening prospect."

"My lungs are fine," she replied, sighing deeply to make the point. He felt he wasn't getting through to this old lady and could see his commission slowly slipping away. It was time to change tack.

"I noticed that part of your property includes a Martello Tower," he said, standing up and looking down at her.

"Conway Tower," she corrected. "After Field Marshal Henry Seymour Conway, a governor of Jersey. It was built in 1781 and funded by King George III. Best military defense of its day with its loopholes, magazine store and machicolations," she said, smiling into her cup.

"Yes, of course, a Conway Tower. How interesting."

"Because of the damp?" she asked.

"We really want to help you solve the problem, Mrs Forster. Get rid of the damp and gas. Make your home habitable," he replied enthusiastically.

"Habitable!" she exclaimed, glaring at him as she stood and pulled herself up to her full four foot eleven height. He felt like a five year old child caught saying a rude word at school and cleared his throat again.

"I mean - more comfortable - for your last few years." Silence. She was enjoying this! Let him dig himself into a deep, deep hole.

"Would you like to see the tower now?" she asked, gesturing towards a low wooden door, comfortably sitting in an old curved wall.

"Of course, thank you," he replied, eagerly following her into the base of the tower.

He knew that further east, around the coast, Archirondel Tower (he must remember to call it Conway not Martello in future), had been carefully restored and looked quite impressive with broad red and white stripes painted on its seaward wall, but an old woman couldn't possibly have done the necessary repairs on this! "There'll be a lot of work to do in here," he said.

The smell surprised him. Not musty as he had expected, but sweet. A smell he recognised. The kind of smell pervading his Nana's bedroom when he was a little boy. As his eyes grew accustomed to the dim light, he saw rows of bottles and jars, a measuring jug, mortar and pestle, a primus stove with well used enamel saucepans and countless herbs and berries hanging from bits of string.

"Herbal medicine, Apothecary it's called," was the only explanation she gave. She pointed towards three stone steps.

"You can go up, if you like."

He ran his hand over the roughly squared granite wall and stepped onto the first floor with its arched fireplace and hearth and three granite dressed ventilation windows. It too was filled with bottles and smells. Then, climbing up to the second floor, he counted twelve musketry loopholes strategically positioned around the room. Looking out through one of these small slits, he tried to picture the soldiers with their muskets pointing out to sea, waiting for possible invasion, but his thoughts returned to Mrs Forster. She unnerved him and he wondered who the old lady really was. He had presumed they were all the same - the old.

"Go up onto the parapet," she called from below. He complied, climbed through a round hatch in the centre of the vault and was hit by a blast of cold air. The moon was shining now and in the eerie light, the branches of a nearby oak tree looked like gnarled arms extended towards him and on the wind, the sound of pebbles relentlessly honed by the sea, hit his senses. He shivered.

"Enough ventilation for you then?" asked Mrs Forster.

He turned, startled. "I – I didn't think you'd be able to climb up here," he exclaimed.

"I thought not." she said, walking towards him and stretching out her arm. He froze and a wave of fear engulfed him as through his mind, flashed the terrifying image of his body flying off the parapet and crashing to the ground.

"No, no please Mrs Forster, don't…"

"Look at those lights."

Lights! Did she say lights? He wiped his face with sweating hands and opened his eyes. She was looking out across the darkening sea, pointing towards the small shimmering lights on the coast of France.

"Beautiful, aren't they?" she said.

He stared at her, let out an audible sigh of relief and shook his head. "Mrs Forster, I really don't understand you at all."

"No, young man, you don't. You just saw an old woman and thought I wouldn't have a brain, or opinions. With your salesman's patter, you thought you could persuade me to buy something I definitely don't want or need." She turned toward him. "Am I right?" He had nothing to say.

"I've had a long, interesting and eventful life. Learnt a lot about people. You should remember that. You didn't even think that I could climb up to my favourite spot with its wonderful view." She laughed, pulling her cardigan tightly around her. "Well, I'm getting cold. Come on lad, let's have another cup of tea." As she disappeared through the hatch to the floor below, he hesitated, just for a moment. "Yes, why not!" he said.

As they sat by the fire, drinking one of her warming herbal teas, she smiled and asked his name.

"Stephen, but my friends call me Steve."

"Can I call you Steve, or is that reserved for the young?"

"Yes, call me Steve. I'd like that." He cleared his throat and she looked at him expectantly. "Mrs Forster, please can I… Um… Can I…"

"Spit it out, lad! Can you what?"

"Can I come back to see the tower in daylight?"

"As a salesman or Steve?"

"Steve, just Steve"

"Now that I know you, Steve, please come any time you wish."

As he walked home, he knew that there was no commission money for the pub, but now, he really didn't mind at all.

P'TUN 1625

MOZ SCOTT

Moz Scott has a career background in both law and psychology and has published articles on both. She is currently working on *The Fear Machine*, a fantasy adventure novel for children in the 8-11 year reading age group.

P'tun 1625 – By Moz Scott

There was no escape from the whiff of rotting seaweed. Flies swarmed around the stacks of drying vraic, like smoke over bonfires.

No longer home to the Governor of Jersey, the imposing walls of Lé Vièr Châté looked neglected, like the prisoners forgotten inside.

My feet were hot and swollen in Aunt Néné's boots. They had holes in their soles and, like the castle, needed repair. The strap on my wooden casket weighed uncomfortably upon my shoulder. My stride became slower up the hill.

My buckled lip made it hard for me to avoid notice. I wished my simple coif covered more than my hair.

Raché Suthâtre, a St Martinnais woman in widow's dress, came alongside me, with a basket full of knitting. Her skin was as leathery as the bark of an apple tree. She narrowed her eyes at me. "Is that p'tun you're selling, Jénîn de-Lièvre?"

My cheeks felt as if they were on fire.

"I suppose you've been hawking your tobacco to those unfortunate souls in St Brelade," she said disapprovingly, "telling them it's a medicine for the plague. The Royal Court forbade the selling of p'tun a year ago — didn't you hear the

131

announcement in your parish church?" She gazed at my lip. "I suppose women like you don't go to church…"

"I go to church," I mumbled self-consciously. "I've heard nothing in the Bible against p'tun."

"Go back to Grouville and learn to speak." Raché mimicked my speech. "You lisp worse than a St Ouënnais!"

An officer was addressing some guards at the gate of the castle. He turned towards us.

"You see this fortress?" Raché said. "Before his gaoler was made Governor in his place, Sir Walter Raleigh saved it from being torn down. He couldn't save himself, though, after making a fashion out of smoking. That's what happens when you offer people the Devil's weed!"

I cringed at being associated with the Devil. It happened often, thanks to my lip.

"What are you two bickering about?" the officer called to us. He was English and spoke French poorly.

Raché jabbed her finger at me, railing in Jèrriais. Three of the militia slipped me some sous. I fished clay pipes out of my casket. Each was stuffed with tobacco.

Keen to make a sale of her own, Raché dangled a pair of stockings in front of the officer's face. The officer waved them away.

132

"You locals must think we soldiers have more legs than spiders!" he said. "With the harvests over, people come here all day to peddle stockings."

Raché frowned at him. A pock-marked guard hesitantly explained what his commander was saying.

Raché brandished her stockings in her fist. "You should take care who you buy from," she shouted at the men of the militia. "Some people knit on the Sabbath!" She tilted her head in my direction. "And you should have acorns in your pockets, dealing with the likes of her!"

Her eyes blazed at me. "Your mother couldn't have been the only sorceress in your family, Jénîn de-Lièvre."

I felt as if scalding oil had been tipped over me. The Devil takes the form of a hare… I was born with the mark of one. A jury at a Grande Enquête du Pays had found that my mother had coupled with Satan. I pictured my mother being strangled in public, before her body was flung onto flames. The taste in my mouth was as bitter as p'tun.

"As for your aunt," Raché snarled, "how could she not have been a witch to have raised the Devil's seed as her own? Why else did she leave you her house and the five perches on which you grow your p'tun?"

Being reminded of my mother's spinster sister brought me fresh grief. My beloved Aunt Néné had sheltered me after my father refused to accept me as his child. I had watched her die painfully of a fever in the spring.

"Take you and your racket away from here, the pair of you," the officer said brusquely. "We've enough work to do, guarding the lowlife in this prison!"

I hadn't sold enough p'tun to repair Aunt Néné's boots. I broke my tramp back to Grouville and rested my blistered feet. The sea was flooding onto the sand, searching for vraitcheurs. With the vraic harvest over, the tide would need some other victim to drown.

I approached the cottage that I had shared with Aunt Néné. A Centenier and his men were waiting at the porch. The sea's weight crashed upon my limbs.

"Jénîn Lèvre-de-Lièvre," the Centenier said, "I am arresting you for acts of sorcery…"

I stood, trembling, in the Parish Hall. The Centenier read out my neighbours' false claims to the Connétable and six Sermentés. How could Jean Le Creux have seen me dancing naked with other women at Rocque Ber? I had never been there. Why had Francois Hubert sworn that I had cursed his mother before she had died? The long list of lies sucked my voice away, draining me of words.

At the Connétable's direction, the Vingtenier pricked my deformed lip with a needle. He shook his head when it failed to bleed. More evidence against me… I felt a surge of seawater rise through my body. It spilled from my eyes.

I returned to Lé Vièr Châté as its prisoner. The warden led me to a part that smelt like the castle's bowels. He pushed me into a dark stone chamber. Its choking stench made me long for the smell of vraic.

134

Four shadowy figures shrank away from me, as far as their fetters would allow. One of them revealed herself as an imprisoned debtor. "Not only do you require me to pay for this wretched lodging," she screeched at the warden, "you're forcing me to share the company of a witch!"

"We're a prison, not an inn!" the warden said. He slammed the door in response to her screams.

A lice-ridden blanket on the grimy flagstones offered me no slumber. I sat in the damp and the dirt, scratching myself between shivers.

Thoughts flitted, like trapped birds, around my head. Who would help me? Aunt Néné, my protector, was dead. My brothers hated me for robbing them of a mother… and of an inheritance from our aunt.

Invisible fingers clutched at my throat, making it hard to breathe. How many jurors were likely to believe my innocence, in the face of so much slander? Banishment seemed preferable to execution, but would deprive me of the possessions I needed to live. I touched my cloven lip. It would not only be my mother's death warrant.

The scamper of a rat startled me. An accused witch was more like vermin than a debtor — she did not have to pay for her keep — but the coins in my skirt pocket, from the sale of p'tun, would buy me no comforts either. My meagre rations, of musty well water and bread, would barely keep me from starving. I prayed, yet questioned whether God would help me… did God consider me to be Devil's seed too?

I would remain a prisoner of the castle until I pleaded guilty or agreed to be tried. To stay in my cell for long would itself be a death sentence.

The daylight's brightness scorched my eyes. My legs felt shaky. I stumbled in my boots. Their stitching was beginning to unravel.

It was my third time to be marched by the halberdiers to the courthouse in St Helier. The blades glinting at the top of their pikes reminded me of the metal that had beheaded the previous Governor. My gulps of fresh air were my only solace.

I waited my turn to reappear before the Cour de Cattel in a cage in the marketplace, surrounded by the sounds of bartering. Passers-by stared and sneered at me, as if I were a beakless chicken being offered for sale and for slaughter. I envied the man in the nearby stocks. His punishment was no more humiliating than my confinement, yet he knew that he would walk free at the end of it.

The stern faces of the Bailiff and the three Jurats were stony. Before being restored to his lofty position, Jean Herault had been imprisoned for a day, in London, after disputing with the Dean. His pale and gaunt appearance suggested he still was languishing in the Marshalsea.

I nibbled at my fingernails, doubtlessly making myself look even more like a hare.

"You once more have heard the charges against you..." Jean Herault's French was halted: he seemed to find breathing as difficult as I did. "Will you now freely submit your case to the Grande Enquête du Pays?"

136

I could not afford a learned man to speak in my defence. I looked up. "No, Sir..."

Jean Herault's lips tightened. "There can only be one reason why you won't!" he snapped. "You are guilty of these crimes and wish to escape punishment for them."

"No, Sir," I pleaded. "Some landowners are friendly with my brothers, who are not friends to me. They will benefit if I am put to death by inheriting —"

"Anyone whom you can challenge on the grounds of prejudice will not be allowed to try you," the Bailiff said dismissively. He nodded towards a lanky man whom I had seen in the courtroom before. "The Attorney-General will ensure you are tried fairly."

I shook my head miserably, haunted by Raché Suthâtre's words. "P'tun will kill me."

"What do you mean?" Jean Herault said sharply.

My voice continued to quiver. "I do not grow much, Sir, but the soldiers say I cure it the best... If I am condemned to die, the men-in-arms will, perforce, buy p'tun from others. The landowners who would try me would profit from my execution!"

"What do you mean, girl? Don't you know the Royal Court has banned the selling of p'tun?" The Bailiff frowned at the Attorney-General. "Amongst those landowners who are strangers to this woman's brothers," he said, "surely there are eight, in each of the three parishes from which the jury would be drawn, who do not grow p'tun?"

137

Elie de Carteret, the Attorney-General, looked discomfited. "It's a matter of which I have been meaning to speak with you, Sir."

He walked to the bench. I strained to hear his whisper.

"Nearly every landowner in the Island... None admit selling it... Growing tobacco is prohibited in England... Heavy taxes on tobacco from the colonies... Smugglers risk pirates in the Channel... Worth more to farmers than any other crop..."

The colour in Jean Herault's robes looked as if it was leaking into his face. "First, we had to stop Islanders from knitting during the harvests," he stormed. "Now, we must curb them from growing p'tun. Otherwise, there will be no food on this Island at all!"

His disdainful glance made me swallow. "Justice will not allow those who flout the law to try this woman. Centenier, charge her... for the crime of selling p'tun!"

A tide receded from me. It took the coins from my pocket — my fine for selling p'tun — and left me holding onto my life.

Released from the court's custody, I dragged my Aunt Néné's tattered boots through the confusion of the marketplace. I stopped to steady myself and looked back at the court building. The tightness in my throat had gone.

A thought surfaced through the lightness in my head like driftwood from a shipwreck.

P'tun did not help to save the life of Sir Walter but, by the grace of God, it had saved mine.

MIRACLES WILL HAPPEN

SUE DU FEU

Sue du Feu is a writer and filmmaker who comes from Jersey. Her childhood was spent listening to tales of the German Occupation from numerous aunts and uncles and it's no coincidence that the subject matter she writes about most stems from those times. This story is an exception.

Miracles will Happen – By Sue du Feu

They still come to look for the Dean. Dean Mabon. Dean of Jersey and worker of miracles. They all want to see him. Is that why you're here? Are you pilgrims? That's how I started, as a pilgrim and then I met the Dean – changed my life. I don't wonder you've sought him out; his reputation has travelled all over the island - they come from as far away as St Ouen to look for miracles.

It was my life's ambition to go on a pilgrimage to the Holy Land. A journey for God's greater glory – yes, a long journey, a difficult journey, but worth it to see the places where Our Lord walked, and talked, and preached, and taught; it was worth it all right.

Travel you see, it broadens the mind. It opened my eyes all right. I saved for years, knew it was what I wanted to do; anyone would have, given the chance. Some travelled on donkeys, and some in wagons, but most of us walked – all the way to Jerusalem, except when we were on the boat, and then I wished I was walking – but more of that later. I couldn't afford a donkey or a place on a wagon. Everything I owned I carried in my scrip, my bag - the bishop blessed it before I left.

There was quite a ceremony. I was sad to go, I wondered if I'd ever see my family again. They saw me to Gloucester city gates – we were all crying, knowing some never came back. We made crosses made of cloth; they were also blessed by the

140

bishop, and then sewn into our hats and cloaks to protect us. We walked to the coast and sailed to France. The roads were terrible; all big stones - took ages to traverse them.

Do you know how we crossed rivers? No bridges. We waded through the water, and when the rivers were too wide we would get a ferry boat; tiny things they were, made out of a single tree trunk - usually very dangerous. They were rogues, those ferry boat men – rooked us they did, nearly as bad as the robbers and brigands.

We walked in groups a long way each day because we had to find shelter each night and there weren't that many of them along the road. Sometimes we found a monastery, but mostly we stayed in inns, smelly and horrible places with some very strange people in them. All sorts of folks were calling themselves pilgrims then.

Anyway this night, a Thursday I think, we couldn't find anywhere to stay. I was exhausted, so weary, and it was hot. We were coming up to Orléans in France and I knew I couldn't go any further. I fell exhausted at the side of the road and thought I couldn't go on any more. As I told them to leave me, I heard a beautiful voice and a hand reached out for mine. "My dear, give me your hand – we will walk together." I looked up and there framed in the sunshine was him, the Dean of Jersey. I didn't know that then of course, I thought it was Our Lord come to help me. He took my hand so gently and assisted me to a monastery for the night and we prayed together – he was a good man, a wonderful man.

The next day he walked with me and told me all about the island of Jersey. I'd never heard of it. He was kind to me right

141

from the start – it was a pleasure to travel with him. He taught me so much and we prayed together every day. He gave me his cloak when it got cold, he never got cold – he was a man of God.

As we neared Venice, where we were getting a boat for Jerusalem, we saw many miracles: statues wept, and wounds bled. My dean was impressed; he wanted to know all about the miracles; he studied them. He could see that pilgrims would pay to see a miracle and he marvelled at it.

In Venice we waited for a galley to take us to the Holy Land and time passed pleasantly enough in prayer and contemplation. When we got on board what a shock: the stink, the noise and the heat on that boat is almost impossible to describe. The timbers creaked, and the waves crashed all around us; there were storms in the Mediterranean Sea all the way across. So many people, all groaning and being sick at the same time, you had to get out of the way, it got all over your clothes. And the food was disgusting – all maggoty yes, maggots in everything, and no proper drinking water. The best place to be was on deck but you had to pay more to get up there. The Dean could afford it so he was out of the stench and the mess; quite right too. It wouldn't be right for him to be thrown in with the likes of us. He needed time to pray and think. He would say words of encouragement to us each day- an inspiration to us all.

When we eventually got to the Holy Land we went into the city of Jerusalem to visit all the holy sites. We got to the Holy Sepulchre, Jesus's tomb, where hundreds of pilgrims were all wailing and sobbing, and some having ecstatic fits, so overcome they were with emotion, and the Dean was so

142

impressed he declared he would build a tomb just like it when he got back to Jersey. He kept his word; it's here at La Hougue Bie. In Jerusalem there were crowds everywhere and people were trampled underfoot when we tried to get in to see the saint's relics - panic and pandemonium everywhere. We had to make offerings at the shrines; anything would do however small, although the rich amongst us gave silver and gold to help maintain the shrine. The Dean took a great deal of interest in the offerings, marvelling at the amounts collected, saying he could do a lot for his church in Jersey if he could only find a way to get pilgrims to come and give offerings.

He watched people pray for miracles and buy the saint's relics - bits of bone, or a scrap of clothing. I asked him if a miracle had ever happened at his chapel. "No", he said, "I wish it had because it would be for the greater glory of God. Then more people would visit the church, and we could do more good for them." It was about then he started to look more closely at the miracles wherever we stopped. He said: "Annie, we're going to have pilgrimages to La Hougue Bie. Would you like to come to live in Jersey and help?" Me? Coming to work here with Dean Mabon? "Oh yes sir, I'd follow you anywhere… but pilgrims need to see a miracle at the end of the pilgrimage," I said. "And they will, Annie, believe me they will," he replied.

So we started the long journey home; only this time I wasn't going home, I was coming here, to this beautiful island. We travelled back during the winter and it was very cold through the mountains. One night we stopped in a holy village where the villagers had seen a miracle in the church there. At night when people went to pray, the candles on the altar were seen to rise up and float into the rafters, all on their own. It

143

happened to us when we were there, we saw it. Wondrous! I asked how sure he was that the pilgrims would see a miracle when they came to his chapel. He looked thoughtfully at me, and went to pray in the church alone, so I left him there to contemplate the wonders of the Lord.

The next day he told me that while he had prayed, the Virgin Mary had come to him. Yes, he'd seen her in a vision, and she'd told him to get the pilgrims to La Hougue Bie and she would appear to them. He was very excited so when we finally got back here he started work immediately on the sepulchre under the Jerusalem chapel and when it was built he had a statue made of the Virgin Mary. He told me she had appeared to him again in a vision; I've never seen her - she only appears to those worthy of seeing her. Anyhow, she told him how the statue was to be made in a certain way to accept offerings.

I was honoured to help with God's work. My job was to work the arm – when the pilgrims entered the sepulchre I was to stand behind the statue and push her arm up and out to accept money in her palm and then I pulled the arm back on its wire and the money fell through into a bucket lined with cloth so that the pilgrims couldn't hear it. It was a great success at first – the pilgrims thought it was a miracle the way the statue accepted the money and then it disappeared, because it looked like the statue was thanking them for their devout offerings and blessing them, which of course was true in a way. The Dean was grateful for all the offerings so the Virgin Mary must have been gratified too.

After a while the people tired of it; it wasn't enough for them. Very fickle are pilgrims, some of them just want a bit of a show and never mind the praying. Dean Mabon worried about how he could keep the interest going for he told me we needed the money now for the good of the parish. Then, one morning he came rushing in to tell me the Virgin Mary had appeared to him again that very night with the answer – we must, with her blessing, tell people that miracles would take place on certain days. He said she'd told him exactly what to do and that I was to have a part in it. I was thrilled. The Virgin Mary wanted my help! Of course the Dean did all the hard work and praying. That's why it was a success.

The Virgin Mary had explained to the Dean how to do the miracle with rising candles we had seen in France. Good of her to take the trouble so that we could do it too. We ran a wire up through the wicks, and it was a thin wire so it couldn't be seen once the candles were lit, disguised by the smoke. I hid and he would give me the signal when the crowds were in the chapel. Then I would start pulling in the wires –and they rose up to the ceiling slowly. You should have seen their faces, and listened to the voices sobbing and wailing and praying as they watched our own miracle at La Hougue Bie.

The Dean was pleased with the offerings the pilgrims left and we performed the miracle every week for a while, but then the pilgrims, fickle lot, stopped coming, complained the miracles weren't real. The Dean said the real reason was because of the Reformation. All this persecution: no-one's allowed to be a Catholic now, or believe in miracles or the Virgin Mary either, more's the pity.

Of course it made my Dean depressed because he couldn't help the parish any more. Sadly, he had to join the Reformers, when I know that's not where his heart lies. He hardly ever comes out of the house now except to say mass. He used to

145

love the crowds and the offerings but now he prays on his own. I look after him, keep house for him. I won't desert him like those pilgrims; I'll always be there for him.

God bless him – and us all.

THE WEDDING GIFT

TESS JACKSON

Tess Jackson spends her time between her homes in Jersey and South Africa. She writes contemporary and historical romance.

The Wedding Gift – By Tess Jackson

It was going to be a very stressful day. My granddaughter's wedding. The heat and humidity was already making my hair damp at the nape of my neck. No time to dilly dally. Even though I'm eighty-one-years-old and in very good health, it takes me a lot longer to look my best. I had no intention of letting the side down.

Jessica is my favourite. Maybe it's because she reminded me of myself as a girl, with her black hair and sparkling blue eyes. She's taller than me though, and very athletic. Jessica was captain of her hockey team at University. That's where she met Mark Lawrence, her fiancé. Such a tall, handsome young man and just the sort I liked when I was young, with his fair hair and green eyes. They will make a handsome couple today. I would look forward to going, if only they had chosen a different venue.

"Gran what are you talking about?" she'd asked. "Of course I want you at my wedding. Why would you think otherwise? I'm so excited, and you know how much this means to Mum. Bye Gran," she said, refusing to listen to further doubts from me. "See you at the wedding." She'd rung off before I could say another word.

That was Jess: happy, flamboyant, panache for the dramatic. One couldn't help loving her, with her flare for making people laugh and her exaggerated storytelling. I, on the

148

other hand, was shy and unsociable. A romantic, even though so many of my dreams are just that, dreams. One can dream at any age, getting old doesn't change that.

It was time to concentrate on getting ready. Alice, my eldest daughter, has put everything ready on a hanger on the outside of the wardrobe. She even hung my long string of pearls over the beautiful pale lilac silk frock and matching jacket. I refused to wear one of those ridiculous fascinators or whatever they call them. More like wearing a dead bird on one's head. I suspect she thinks I can't remember which outfit she wants me to wear. There's nothing wrong with my memory. Sometimes I wish there was and then it wouldn't matter that they had chosen Mont Orgueil Castle for their wedding venue. I tried to talk them out of it, but was outvoted. They couldn't know why I had such an aversion to going back to that castle.

If only the young could know how we had suffered during the Occupation. The German soldiers did some horrendous things to the prisons of war. They garrisoned Mont Orgueil castle, building lookout posts to cover the sea all the way across to the French coast. It was out of bounds to us children, and any other Islanders for that matter.

I was ten-years-old. Peter my brother was three years older. Mother would send us out to collect wood or twigs from Grouville common because the coal had long run out. There was little food to be had. The farmers nearby were very kind and gave us whatever they could spare from their meagre rations. I remember the soup tasting of hot onion water. I still can't eat onions, and hate soup.

The winter of 1944 was bitterly cold. One afternoon Peter and I went foraging for anything we could eat, or that would burn. We hoped to maybe find a rotting cabbage that the farmer had left in his field. Rain and wind lashed against our threadbare coats as we walked. Our fingers blue with cold, protruded from worn-out gloves. We had walked all the way to castle green, from Grouville, where we stopped to huddle from the rain against the great wall of Mont Orgueil Castle. My teeth were chattering and I was crying with the cold. Peter insisted we couldn't return home without finding something to take back home for mother.

Suddenly we heard the roar of engines. Six German soldiers came over the hill on their motor bikes and passed just in front of us as they made for the castle entrance. We watched as huge doors opened and a guard came out to await a car that had been following the bikes. The motor bikes disappeared inside while the car stopped at the entrance. The guard opened the car door and dragged out a dishevelled man wearing handcuffs. The prisoner's face was swollen on one side and there was blood on his tattered shirt. I started to scream. I always hated the sight of blood, no matter whose it is.

Peter put his hand over my mouth, but not before the guard had heard and glanced across to where we were hiding. We watched as he said something we couldn't hear to the driver, who jumped out. We ran, but he screamed at us to halt. Peter was dragging me by the hand but I tripped and fell. Two big rough hands caught me, pulling me up by my long plait. I screamed and kicked, yelling at him to put me down.

"Leave my sister alone, you brute," Peter shouted, kicking the soldier on the shin. With that the man let go of my hair and

150

gave poor Peter a hard slap across his head sending him flying. The guard hearing all the commotion yelled for backup and out ran two more soldiers, both carrying guns.

We were terrified. Each guard approached and grabbing us by the arms they dragged us into the castle. The big doors clattered closed. The Nazis were talking to each other in raised voices and very quickly, but having had to learn their language at school, Peter understood some of what they were saying.

"They're going to throw us over the parapets with that prisoner who they say stole from them and tried to escape." He lowered his voice further. "He's been on the run for a week."

"You can't just kill us, we didn't do anything wrong," Peter shouted, trying to sound brave. "Our dad will kill you if you do us any harm."

I'd never seen my brother so upset and angry and it upset me further.

The men looked at us with our streaming eyes and red noses and roared with laughter. It was a big joke to them, deliberately letting us think we would be killed. They had obviously expected one of us to understand some of their words.

The prisoner shouted at them to leave us alone and the guard closest to him beat him with the butt of his rifle. Blood oozed out of his head. I fainted. When I awoke it was to find Peter holding my hand, saying over and over how sorry he was for bringing me to the castle.

Moments later, bored with their entertainment, they unceremoniously pushed us through the small gate at the entrance. Peter took me by the hand and we ran to the edge of the green, where we stopped to catch our breath.

The rain had stopped. Looking back we could see the guards holding the prisoner over the side of the tallest tower. If they let go, he would be killed on the rocks below. I screamed and Peter pulled my face into his skinny chest, whispering at me not to look. I blocked my ears when I heard a scream. I struggled away from him to look back up to the parapet. We couldn't see the prisoner and I was certain they'd let him crash to his death.

Peter and I made a pact that we would never tell anyone about what happened that day. We never did. Even my late husband, Stan, never heard the full story. I wonder now whether it was my imagination that had made me hear the prisoner fall onto the rocks.

Sadly my brother died nine years ago. I wish he could have been with me today, as only he understood what horrors Mont Orgueil Castle held for me. I decided to phone Jessica. I dialled the number and let the phone ring six times. Seven. Eight.

"Is that you, Grace?" a deep voice asked.

"Yes, Mark."

"You sound worried. Is anything the matter?"

I hesitated briefly. "Would Jess be very upset if I don't make the wedding? I feel a little off colour," I said.

"If you don't come to our wedding there'll be a hell of a fuss from your granddaughter," he said sounding upset. "Knowing Jess, she might even cancel. You have to be there, Grace. Please." He rang off and I stared at my wrinkled hands with my fresh manicure.

Enough. Perfume, that's what I needed. Shalimar would make me feel happy. I was a mood person when it came to perfume. I had a different perfume to enhance every feeling depending on how I felt and what I had to do for the day.

Dressed, my hair immaculate and jewellery on, I looked at myself in the mirror. I actually liked what I saw. Today was not about me though, it was about these two young people in love.

"You can do this," I said to my reflection, perfecting my smile in the mirror.

My daughter Alice had given me strict instructions to be ready by eleven o'clock for the taxi's arrival. Jessica will be leaving with her father soon after. Alice has insisted on coming to get me from my cottage, I think she wants to check me out before we leave. I hope she likes the way I look. Young people have such different ideas these days, as to how we should dress.

The castle was bathed in sunlight as the taxi arrived and parked in the delegated area. Stepping carefully onto a manicured lawn, I watched beautiful people mingling as they made their way to the chapel. I looked up at the ramparts that had haunted me all my life.

"Mum, why are you looking over there? Jessica will be here with her dad any minute," Alice said. "We need to get seated." Without a word I obediently followed my daughter.

Jessica looked breathtakingly beautiful as she walked towards Mark, both smiling. Her father gave her hand to the man she loved. Her younger sisters, dressed in the same lilac as my outfit, looked angelic. Flowers adorned the area. Sun streamed through the windows and danced on the young couple as they made their vows. Silly old woman that I am, I felt a tear rolling down my wrinkled cheek.

Lunch was served in another large room, again decorated with candles and flowers. My son-in-law had spared no expense with the food and wine. I don't drink anything but champagne these days though. It's the whim of an old lady and I do it because I can.

Is it the champagne, or my vivid imagination, I wonder, seeing my brother Peter smiling at me from where he stands behind Jessica at the top table. I watch as he turns and walks across the room. At the door he turns and waves to me. I raise my hand and give him a knowing smile.

"Who are you smiling at Mum?" my daughter asks, giving me a puzzled look, as she follows my gaze to the exit.

"Take no notice of me, Alice. I'm just an old woman who thought she saw her long deceased brother. It's probably a trick of the light and wishful thinking."

"Sure you should be drinking?" she asked in a worried tone.

I just nodded and smiled as sweetly as I know how.

It turned out to be a glorious afternoon. Everyone moved to the terrace overlooking Grouville bay and the golf course. I stood looking at the young newly-married couple and mused at how fortuitous it was that they had chosen this venue after all.

Unbeknown to them, they'd given me a gift and it seems that finally both Peter and I have put our demons to rest.

Mammoth

Jon Hackwood

Jon Hackwood was born in North Yorkshire and moved to Jersey in 1987. He is new to writing and Jon has written his first short story for this anthology.

Mammoth – A Neanderthal hunt – By Jon Hackwood

It was my twelfth summer when our village set out on the hunting party. I had been held entranced by stories of the hunters and their exploits across the marshlands. The high lands across the marshlands were long known for the abundance of mammoth and rhino which had sustained our village over winter for generations.

The hunting party was made up of twenty of the strongest hunters and twenty of us novices. For some of us, like me, it will be our first hunt. For others, although not accepted as hunters it will be the second or third hunt. Most bear the scars and carry the stories of previous hunts.

The village had spent time renewing the spears, clubs and hand axes needed to fell these beasts. The womenfolk and the village would be guarded during our absence by those not old enough to join the hunt and those trusted warriors who had experienced many a hunt in the past.

Along with our spears and clubs we had a couple of large bachins and cooking tools. The bachins will be used for cooking and a special purpose, which I was to find out about later.

After arriving at the high lands we made camp near the cave, which would be our base for the hunt. The cave, known as Cotte, is located at the end of a finger of high land leading to the marshes. The Cotte would be a store for the bounty of the hunt and for the hunting party should any large cats get the scent of the meat.

Once the camp was set up it was time for our last meal of the day. This consisted of dried meat and roots cooked in the bachin with fresh water from the nearby spring. I had been sent to collect wood for the first fire. The following morning I would be sent further into the high lands to collect the animal waste that we would use.

The second day started with the rising of the sun and the sounds of birds, as normal. The remains of last evening's meal would give us the energy for our tasks, until the hunters could bag us some small game for the rest of the hunt.

Those of us not yet accepted as hunters were sent to collect supplies. The easy part was collecting the wild flax we needed to make the extra ropes. The hard part was the collection of the animal waste to be burnt to make the seallac. The seallac would be used to stop meat from the hunt going bad before we could get it back to our village. There was a second use for the seallac but I wouldn't find out about that until after the first hunt.

Back at the camp the fires were built up and some novices were sent to collect seawater. When they returned they also brought a selection of sea fish and shells that would make a change from meat and the roots.

The seawater was emptied into the bachins on the fires, and after a short time the water started to smoke. This was the first time I had seen this happen. The more the water smoked the lower it got in the bachin until there was nothing left but a white crystal powder. This is the seallac, I was told. The bachin was emptied out and refilled with seawater to produce more of the seallac. We needed as much as we could make, almost the same size as a small hut back at the village.

After watching the seallac making for a time I was called to help with rope making. The wild flax we had collected was beaten upon a rock to make it split. We then wove parts of the wild flax together to make long ropes. The ropes were left out in the sun to dry and harden as they have to be strong to help with the hunt.

After a hard day's toil we sat around the camp fire and the hunters entertained and scared us with their stories of previous hunts. Watching the flickering of the flames and listening to the stories had my head spinning with pictures of the beasts we would face over the rest of our time on the high lands.

The dawning of the new day brought more new experiences for me. Today I was to go out with the hunting party to find the animals we had come to the high lands for. It was not necessary to kill any of the largest animals on this trip, simply to find out where they are. So, taking with us dried meat and water carriers, we set off for the day, ten hunters and ten of us younger members to learn. The high lands are not as big as our home lands but it would take us more than three days to explore, returning each night to our camp site near the Cotte.

The first day's exploration took us to the pastures closer to our home lands. We stopped at the tomb of some of the ancestors to ask for help in our search and success with the hunt when it came. The tomb could be seen for a way off as we walked over land that was unknown to me. Once we made it, the tomb itself was at the base of a large earthen mound, which only the elders of our group were to enter.

We progressed further into the pasture lands and could see several of the mammoths and rhinos that we looked for. As we approached them, with the wind in our faces, I was struck by the size and the noise of the beasts. Having heard the hunters stories my imagining had not prepared me to see the beasts in the flesh. I first thought that the stories of the giant four legged beasts had been wrong, as I saw before me what looked like creatures with five legs. The more we followed them the more I saw that they actually had a long nose which they would use to pluck the grass and herbs they ate.

As we tracked the beasts we novices were tasked with collecting their waste to heat our fires back at camp. We learnt to use this as well to hide us from their long noses that would smell the air around them. The noise they made reminded me of the thunder from distant storms or the sound that could be made when blowing through a large sea shell.

All the way back to our camp my head was buzzing with what I had seen of the beast we were here to hunt. Whether it was the visit to our fathers at their tomb, or the thoughts of what was yet to come, my sleep was filled with visions.

Over the next couple of days the winds were blowing from the wrong area of the sky so activity was based around the camp. The ropes were dry and gathered ready for the hunt, more of the seallac was made, together with spears and arrowheads ready for the time we would set out for the hunt.

After we had been in the high lands for fourteen days and nights we were awoken early - the wind was blowing in the right direction... We set out towards the homelands in two groups: ten hunters and five novices in each group. The remaining ten strongest novices stayed back near camp, ready for the end of the hunt.

When we arrived at the tomb of our father the two groups split in two directions. One heading back towards camp, through the pastures, and the one I was with heading further into the high land pasture to get behind the herds. As we progressed we used the beasts' waste to hide from their noses before we got ready and were close enough.

As we came nearer the herd I could smell the beasts and hear them rip the grass and herbs from the ground. When we were close enough to throw a spear at the beasts we jumped out of the grasses and threw spears and stones to get the beasts to move towards our camp. As the beasts saw the hunting party they sounded alarm and turned in the direction we wanted them to run.

We chased after them collecting the spears and rocks as we ran. My chest was thumping and my breath became quick. We kept picking up spears and rocks, throwing them toward the beasts to keep them running. Some of our better hunters could make the target and the beasts ran on with spears attached.

As we continued the hunt we saw our other group ahead. They rushed toward the beasts to make them turn the way we wanted, towards our camp. As the beasts turned some of the novices and an experienced hunter ran close to the beasts feeling the sting of tusks as the beasts turned their heads wildly. But none fell. As the beasts turned and continued to run we came nearer and nearer to our camp and to the drop off of land that was our target.

The closer we came to the drop off of land, the more the beasts became aware of it so the more we would throw our spears and rocks to keep them moving. At the edge of the drop off, one of the beasts turned to avoid it. The next was not as quick and its feet were lost underneath it as it fell over the edge. At seeing the beast fall the hunters slowed and changed direction to prevent another beast from following. This did not work as a rhino could not slow enough to miss the drop off and followed the mammoth that had fallen.

As we reached the edge of the drop off we could see the beasts on the land below surrounded by the rest of our strongest novices. The novices were quick to act and used their spears to finish off the mammoth and the rhino that had fallen. The ropes were used to tie the legs and the beasts died quickly. As the main hunting party we made our way safely to the lower land and our camp.

The group elders used a little of the seallac on the cuts of the hunter and novices who had been too close to the tusks of the mammoth during the hunt. The rest of us collected our stone axes and a bachin and headed to the dead beasts. The bachin was used to collect the blood of the mammoth, some of which was used to mark us novice hunters as men of our tribe. The rest of the blood was carried back to camp for later.

The axes and spears were used to cut into the beasts, removing the legs and the rump to return with us to our homelands. The same was done to the rhino all the while the

162

birds gathered to take their chance. One of the elder hunters used a hand knife to cut open the belly of both the mammoth and the rhino, and removed a large reddish brown part of each beast. This was to be our prize meal that evening, cooked with the blood and the roots we had collected earlier in our trip.

I would live to see many more hunting parties to the high lands and would take my own sons with me on their first. None of the hunts would ever match the memory of my first, which has stayed with me for my lifetime.

HER DAUGHTER
AT THE DOLMENS

PAUL BISSON

Paul Bisson is a teacher, writer and musician. His novels *Coyote Jack and the Bluebirds* and *Marigold Dark* are available for purchase on Amazon.

Her Daughter at the Dolmens – By Paul Bisson

"Look at the camera, poppet. Arms in the air for mummy. Arms in the air."

But Celia isn't listening. Celia has found something small and colourful in the dune grass, something infinitely more wonderful than this drab arrangement of stones at which they've stopped. Having curled down into a pigtailed question mark she now has the little coloured thing in her hand.

"Oh darling, please put it down!"

What is that, a discarded cough sweet? An item of dropped jewellery? Annabelle is about to snatch it from her daughter when Celia rears up, treasure held aloft.

"Lego, mummy! Someone's dropped their Lego!" She laughs, her voice spiralling upwards with delight. From here Annabelle can make out the little amber cube in the girl's hand. It's one of those translucent ones you get in the modern sets. God knows she's plucked enough of them from the underflesh of her foot.

"Well put it down dear. You don't know where it's been." Dog's bum, whispers her brain. "The same ubiquitous dog's bum against which everything her daughter plucks from public land has most probably been brushed." Annabelle tries to smile at the irrationality of the notion, though she's too tetchy for smiling today, too pressed for time. "Come stand between those two dolmens so Mummy can take her shot. We've not got long."

They haven't. Kate and Meredith will be getting to the spa at one; Annabelle is damned if she's going to sacrifice herself on the altar of their gossip by being the last one there. It's going to be tight though, especially now that Annabelle's mother has requested Celia be dropped to her door instead of handed over in the Co-op car park as originally planned. There's just time to get these few shots of Her Daughter at the Dolmens snapped and uploaded to Facebook and then they must be heading back to the Range Rover and away from the sand dunes, coloured Lego bricks or not.

"Please Celia." Annabelle feels the sweat prickling her brow. The day is hot, the azure sky cloudless; summer is in full swing. "Stand over there with your arms stretched out like a flower. Remember what I told you about the elves that live here. If you're lucky they'll come and settle on your arms."

Invisible elves, of course, the sort that Celia won't be able to see, but what's the harm in this little white lie? Let's face it; fat men in red suits squeezing sacks of presents down the chimney, fairies that come and take away your used teeth, angry men in the sky that punish you if you don't say your prayers... life's full of such nonsense. Where's the wonder in a fib-less world? As her husband Charles is fond of saying. Indulge a little. Fill their heads with magic and mystery before reality clouts it from their ears.

All very well, thinks Annabelle, were it not me that's so often left to do the filling. She's half a mind to call him up, interrupt his latest jaunt to the City, ask him have a go at persuading Celia to do what she's told for a change. But no; he's probably enjoying the magic and mystery of some important lunch right now, sipping wine with the financial fairies and expense-winged elves upon which their comfortable life in Jersey depends.

Comfort. Of all the words in Annabelle's lexicon (which is sizeable; she didn't get a first in English Literature all those years ago through sheer luck alone) the word 'comfort' is the one that fills her with the greatest unease. At times she views it as a command; 'come, fort', an invitation to her material possessions to gather round like a walled fortress, protecting, securing, shielding her from the worry that must plague the lower sections of society, or All Those Without, as she occasionally catches herself tagging them, with some small degree of shame.

And yet it gets lonely in this fortress of hers. As necessary as she deems it to be, her Com-Fort can be isolating, especially when Charles is away. Karina's English is limited, and once the cleaner has left for the day Annabelle often finds herself staring out over the fields from the conservatory, cigarette in hand (with Celia upstairs in front of CeeBeebies or Frozen – she'd never smoke in front of her daughter) staring and smoking and wondering whether she'd built her Com-Fort too high, longing for the occasional breach in its walls.

Silly, really. Annabelle is one of the lucky ones. She knows this. Out here amidst the rugged, undulating sprawl of the sand dunes she is suddenly grateful for the solid home awaiting her, the cigarettes in the cupboard, the small oak bar Charles had installed on a whim with its ever-winking array of tea-time treats. Things could be worse.

"Celia, darling. For the love of god. Please. Just…just stand there between these two rocks. Arms out like a flower. One photo, that's all. For Mummy."

Rocks? She'd called them dolmens earlier, assuming from the position of the mottled granite boulders – five in all, two pinkish blocks rising vertical to waist height, three laid flat behind to form a crude rectangle – that these were laid here by design. And to be out here like this at the base of the largest hillock on the dunes; what else could they be if not dolmens, lugged here by some determined Neanderthal glad to be free of the grim-set wife left pacing around the family cave?

Annabelle checks the time on her phone. Half past eleven. She's going to be late. Meredith's knives will be glinting. Whose stupid idea was this anyway, coming out here to the dunes like this?

"Maltesers, mummy! I found Maltesers!"

"For god's sake Celia, don't touch that!" shouts Annabelle, causing Celia to leap away from the rabbit droppings towards which her fingers had briefly quested.

Whose idea indeed? Hers, of course. A response to the those naggings of conscience first occasioned by Meredith's recently uploaded Facebook album of Danny and Liv at Gorey Castle, the whole schmaltzy 'culturing up the kids' trend that seemed to be spreading like a virus amongst her friends. First it had been Meredith – Danny sat astride a cannon, Liv grinning

168

up at a waxwork cavalier – with Kate swiftly following suit and carting her three off to La Hougue Bie for some oh-so-cutesy shots inside the burial chamber and all that King of the Castle stuff on the top of the mound.

The Kids Getting to Know Their Island! Kate had posted, each perfectly framed shot more a testament to the unerring beauty of her children (of course!) then a signal of any genuine interest in the Jersey's past.

The comments that followed had set Annabelle's teeth grinding. Good for you, Kate and your little historians. Bless them xx. And of course Helen had to get in on the act, her grammar wince-inducing as always: "so important that they no about there island. Mine are off to Elisabeth Castle at the wknd".

Yes, heritaging was order of the day at the moment, and so here Annabelle was, phone in hand, trying to get her daughter to pose for just one half-decent shot amongst these bloody dolmens...

"Ossuary."

Annabelle turns, startled at the man's voice. It wouldn't be fair to say that he's crept up on them - Annabelle's been staring into the screen of her mobile and must simply have missed his approach from the car park – yet still his sudden presence unnerves her.

"I'm sorry?"

"The Ossuary. These standing stones here. That's what they're called."

169

He's in his fifties, bald on top yet sporting a bushy grey moustache and beard. Like her he's sweating, dark patches ringing the armpits of a faded yellow t-shirt, the bottom of which is tucked into a pair of khaki shorts. A rucksack is strapped tightly to his back.

Annabelle's not quite sure what your average paedophile is supposed to look like these days – there seems to be so many of them about – but there's a guileless excitability to the man's voice and movements that she finds moderately reassuring. An eccentric, certainly, though she and Celia are most probably safe. Still, she can't resist an anxious glance down at his socks, which are hoisted full and rumple free to his knees.

"What's an oss-u-wary?" Pipes Celia. Instinctively Annabelle takes a small step to her right, inserting herself directly between the man and her daughter.

"A place to put human bones, my dear," says the man, pushing his glasses up onto the bridge of his nose with his index finger. "They found a load of them here. At least twenty skeletons, or parts of them at least."

"Really, I…" Annabelle begins, though Celia cuts her off.

"Did people die here?"

"A long time ago," says the man. "Back in Neolithic times. Way before you were born." He flashes Annabelle a wink. "And Mummy too, I'm guessing."

Annabelle glances anxiously over the man's shoulder in the direction of the car park. A hundred metres or so of pocked, gorse-swept terrain separates them from the Range Rover and escape. And should she need to cry for help? There are some people over there, on the rim of that sand crater, though too far away to be of any use.

"Did the dinosaurs eat them?"

"Oh no, the dinosaurs were long gone by then. No, this is simply where they buried their dead. Bright young thing, isn't she?" The man smiles at Annabelle, displaying wonky teeth.

"Um...yes."

"I used to teach her age back when I had a use." He hooks his thumbs under the straps of his rucksack. "'What is she...four? Five?"

"Four. Just turned. You used to be a teacher?" Annabelle feels her anxieties lift. Of course – the man has all the appearance of a spent teacher; probably a geography specialist or some such. The beard. That horrible rucksack. The complete lack of sartorial awareness. How silly of her to worry.

"A good few years back. Gave it all up though to write books."

"On what?"

"On these things." The man nods down at the stones. Dolmens. Ossuary. Whatever. "Neolithic burial sites. Fascinating topic, you know. And Jersey's got some great ones. This must be my sixth visit? No, seventh. I think. You know the..."

171

"So what did eat them then?" Celia has wondered over to the stones and now stands between the two tallest, arms outstretched so that her palms are resting on the tops of each. It's a perfect photo pose, and yet Annabelle hesitates for fear of appearing... what? Disrespectful? Crass?

"Probably nothing," continues the man. "Most likely they just died and were buried here by their Neolithic friends."

"But it's lonely out here," says Celia. "Wouldn't they get lonely out here?" Annabelle's hands twitch; the iPhone raises itself as if by magic, her daughter and the dolmens filling the screen in perfect frame. It really is a lovely shot.

"Oh I don't know about that," continues the man, clearly in his element. "You see once you're dead you're dead, my dear. And once the bones had been excarnated there was little else to be done but to offer them back to the earth from which they came."

Annabelle feels a sudden flare of panic in her guts. Bones, death and burial; these aren't concepts she wants rattling around her daughter's brain. Elves and fairies, yes. These? No.

She goes to speak, yet already Celia has cut her off.

"What's a carnation?"

"Ex-carnation. They used to lay the corpses out in the open air so that animals and birds could pick the bones clean of flesh. Only then would they be buried. You see, Neolithic man believed that..."

172

"Celia darling," blurts Annabelle, reaching out for her daughter. "Time to go."

But Celia isn't listening. Instead she drops to the floor and rolls over to lie face up amidst the boulders, her arms spread wide. "Take a picture, Mummy!" She implores. "I'm a carnation! The animals have eaten me! Take a picture!"

"Celia!" Annabelle barks, her iPhone forgotten. She moves in to scoop her daughter from the space between the stones yet for some reason her limbs freeze; she dare not step within. Instead she can only yell her daughter's name, commanding her to get up and come, get up and come with her this instant, right now.

"But I'm a carnation, mummy! Take my picture! I'm a carnation in my oss-u-wary!"

"CELIA!"

"Oh what a bright young thing!" laughs the man. Pushing his glasses up to the bridge of his nose he leans in as Celia giggles and squirms within her tiny granite chamber, her bare arms raised to the sky. "Such a very bright thing indeed!"

SEA BRIDE

HOWARD DANIELS

Howard Daniels took up writing short stories and articles when he retired from teaching. He has won several prizes in both the Guernsey and Jersey Eisteddfods. More recently, one of his stories appeared in Jersey Now.

Sea Bride – By Howard Daniels

"Did you know Harry Potter hated summer holidays, Tony?"

"It's such a glorious sunny August day. And we've just been surfing in St. Brelade's Bay. I don't see how Harry Potter could possibly hate summer holidays, do you?"

"It's because he was a wizard. It says so in this book, Harry Potter and the Prisoner of Azkaban."

"So wizards don't like summer, eh Sue?"

"No, they like dark, sinister places and black magic."

"Like La Cotte cave we climbed to yesterday? Where they discovered fossils of mammoth tusks and skeletons? The one we found all walled up and couldn't get into? That's amazing! You're a local Jersey girl and an archaeologist. I bet you could tell me many a strange story about these places. I'd love to hear them."

"Well, where would you like me to start? There are so many. The Channel Islands aren't called 'The Enchanted Islands' for nothing. If you look on some of the old Jersey granite houses like the ones you saw at St. Aubins, you'll see steps on the chimney stacks. These are where witches rest in their nightly flights. Oh yes, Tony, believe me. There's magic in the air, even on a hot summer's day. You'd better watch out!"

"You're bewitching me already."

"I could tell you about brave Lord Hambrye, who slew the dragon that guarded the Neolithic burial mound at La Hougue Bie. Or the Black Dog with Saucer Eyes? That was the famous Black Dog that terrorised the area in the seventeenth century. Some say the dog was just invented by smugglers trying to keep prying eyes away from their nefarious activities on the lonely coast. But, although nobody had ever reported ever having seen it, it was thought to be very scary.

"Or perhaps you'd like to hear about the three sirens of Rocqueberg, who conjured up storms to drive sailors onto the rocks below? If you like, I can take you to see the Devil's hoofmark still embedded in the rock where the witches practised their wicked spells and had sex with the Devil.

"Then there's the charming tale of the wicked kelpie at Bonne Nuit Bay, who tried to take a human bride by night when the moon was full. He tricked her into going with him by taking the form of her soldier lover. Then he stirred up the sea to boiling pitch and dragged her under the raging waves. It's a good story, but somehow I don't think you'd like it."

"They all sound most exciting. That last one sounds much too horrible! But I'm intrigued by that headland over there. I'd like to hear the legend of La Cotte. Please tell me what happened and why it's walled up."

Sue let her book fall open onto the sand and started to comb her long fair hair.

"It's an odd story to tell on such a lovely summer's day, but, if you want, here goes.

176

Oh, it all took place long, long ago – about three centuries ago, actually. It's only a winters' tale, but, you know, in the past Jersey folk were very superstitious – and even today there are some who believe in such beings as Silkies, half-human, half sea-creatures. Perhaps you've heard of them?"

Tony nodded. "In Celtic mythology there are many such tales."

Sue gave him a whimsical smile. "Perhaps you'll believe this story too by the time I've finished."

"Go on then. I'd love to hear it."

"Dark and cold was that night. The wind blowing around Ouaisné Bay was a freezing, biting, bitter wind, a foreboding wind, a wind of evil, harbinger of death and disaster. The hungry waves lashed the barren rocks and thundered into the echoing chasm known as La Cotte. As the tide at its height billowed and foamed into the cave, dragging weed and shingle up and down, it bore something else as well - something that was to change a simple fisherman's life forever.

In his lonely whitewashed cottage, perched precariously on the headland above Ouaisné, Jean de la Cour snuggled deeper under his rough blanket as the rain lashed the window.

'Tis the devil of a night to be out at sea fishing,' he said to himself.

Tomorrow he would go to his boat below. He'd made it as secure as possible, but the storm was the worst he'd ever experienced. Lazily he reached for the candle and snuffed it out. Then through his slumbers he thought he heard a plaintive voice, calling, summoning him to rise from his bed and go out into the cold dawn.

The morning dawned grey and misty, but the storm had abated and the sea had subsided. His boat had gone. A few gulls were wheeling forlornly around, hungry for food. It was no use searching the deserted beach.

Desperately he clambered over the rocks, grasping, falling and cutting himself in his haste. On round the point of the headland he scrambled, until he found himself at the entrance to La Cotte. Fortunately the tide was low, so he was able to enter the cave. The floor rose steeply and rocks and debris hindered his progress. He hoped he would find his boat inside.

Then once more he heard that plaintive beckoning voice. It sounded like a song, rising and falling in perfect harmony with the ebb and flow of the tide. To the sound of obscure harmonies there floated into the cave all the dreams and memories of the Land Beneath the Waves. It was a siren call, impelling him gently yet firmly to go forward to find the singer. As he drew nearer he could make out the words; words sung so enchantingly that his young heart beat faster and faster.

Oh ye Tritons, Naiads, Creatures of the Deep,

Find me a home where my soul may sleep

Oh trident-bearing Neptune, King of the Dolphins, Lord of the Great Abyss,

I humbly beseech ye to grant me today my greatest wish.

Send me this day

Someone to love, cherish and obey.

Then Jean saw the Sea Nymph. She was combing her long golden tresses with a silver comb. Her gorgeous locks cascaded over her naked body down to her waist. Jean gazed enraptured, enthralled by her ethereal beauty. Little did he heed or even remember the stories his dead mother had told him when he was a child; fabulous tales of the creatures of the deep who lure men's souls, take their spirits and cast their dying bodies on the shore for rabid seabirds to pick the bones. He heeded not the sealskin coat, now cast off, lying on the rock beside her. Jean De La Cour was madly, passionately, wholly, completely, utterly head-over-heels in love – and no mortal in the whole wide world could change this, his first fine careless rapture.

He rushed forward and knelt beside her, there on the cold hard ground, as the mists of morning faded and the sun filtered into the cave, filling it with warmth and love.

The maiden stopped singing, then gracefully bent her slender neck towards him. As their lips touched, they knew that they would love each other for the rest of their lives.

Jean and Melusene – for such was the name of the sea-maiden – were married in St. Brelade's Church and great was their joy and happiness. There were not many guests, for Jean's parents were both dead and he had few relatives.

As they walked hand-in-hand out of the church, they noticed a small bag lying on the steps. Inside was the most beautiful collection of shells they had ever seen. From the deepest depths of the ocean were elegant pink and yellow conch shells, from the South Pacific smooth brown and white

179

striped cowries and antler coral: beautiful fan-shaped scallops and best of all, the coiled Nautilus.

'Oh how lovely!' exclaimed Melusene.

It was only later that they found the note inside:

'A gift to you on your wedding day. Do not forget your bargain with Neptune, King of the Oceans.' In the excitement of the wedding day, Jean did not grasp the significance these words would have in the future.

Days and months of idyllic happiness passed on silken wings. On the golden evenings of warm summer, when the wavelets chuckled and danced under the rocks and the air was warm with the scent of the gorse from the cliff tops, the couple would swim out into the cool wide sea, planning and dreaming. Melusene would swim and dive with her mate and introduce him to her family down below in the Land beneath the Waves, and they would sport and play together.

Then one night, as the summer evenings slid down to the golden skies of autumn, when they lay contentedly in each other's arms, Melusene revealed to Jean her secret; she was with child. He was overjoyed. But then she reminded him of the bargain she had made with Neptune in order to get his permission to marry Jean; she was to make a sacrifice to the King of the Sea. Somehow they both guessed what that might be.

Not long afterwards the baby was born – little Aurora, and no more beautiful and fair a child was there in the whole land. As she grew up they taught her many things about the sea –

how to dive and swim and chase the dancing moonbeams across the shining water. Their happiness was complete.

Yet sometimes as the years sped by Jean would find Melusene no longer beside him. Then he would go outside to the headland overlooking La Cotte and watch her quietly as she gazed wistfully out to sea, a faraway look on her face. When she turned to him, he saw that her face was wet with tears.

'What is the matter, my darling?' he would say, taking her into his arms.

'I'm so frightened,' she would reply and gently nuzzle against his broad shoulders. But she would never explain any further.

One fatal night, as the gales of winter lashed the headland, Jean awoke to find that Melusene and the child had gone. In vain did he rush out into the storm, lantern swinging in the wind, drenched to the skin, calling, calling her name. In vain did he search the rocks and the barren crags. Then in desperation he flung himself over the cliff edge. Above him rose the waves. Down, down, he went to the deep-sea bottom, where his wife and child were waiting for him.

The next day the winter sun shed its pale rays over a deserted beach. No trace of any bodies was ever found. Neptune's bargain had been repaid."

"What a sad story," said Tony, as he lay back on the hot sand. "What happened to the skeletons they found in the cave?"

"Oh, they found three of them. One male, the second female, and the third that of a child. And the woman's bone structure bore a remarkable resemblance to that of a seal's. That's why the cave's walled up today."

"Well, that certainly made a fitting tomb for Jean de la Cour and his family, didn't it? It's getting late. Let's go and get some tea now. You've bewitched me enough for today."

Later, on that glorious day Tony and Sue sat and watched the sun sink slowly and majestically into the sea beyond Corbière lighthouse, turning the rose-pink granite rocks into blood red. It was then Tony felt Sue's head snuggle onto his shoulder and her fair hair cascade over his cheeks.

Not only has she bewitched me but she has seduced me as well, he thought. She's the most beautiful girl I've ever seen. I shall have to stay in Jersey now.

They both knew at that moment that they were in love and they would never leave each other.

WARM SAND

JULIA HUNT

Julia Hunt is a freelance journalist and editor. She has written news, features and travel articles for a wide range of publications in the UK and beyond. She is the founder of Jersey's first independent restaurant guide and is working on her first novel.

Warm Sand – By Julia Hunt

She hadn't slept properly since it had happened; six months of fractured nights, no dreams, just horrible thoughts, of horrible things. It was the picture which had sold the possibility of escape to her really; a boat that was a house, bedrooms more like cabins, right on the beach.

You could see the house with its glossy cream walls, wrapped in a ribbon of green paint, from miles away across the bay, but, standing just below it, under the high sea wall, it was invisible. Cassandra booked accommodation for a few days; packed a small bag, took a flight. She didn't tell anyone; there wasn't really anyone to tell.

Calling it a barge didn't do it justice. That implied it was moored someplace inland, on a canal in a once industrial city. But this was no Birmingham or Bradford, no Salford or Leeds, not even a Cambridge or an Oxford. This was a beach, opening onto the Atlantic. Its palette wasn't red bricks and grey water, the enclosed shades of a city; it was blue and white, and all shades of sky and sea in between.

The sound of the waves was the best lullaby she knew. Calm or crashing, the sea provided a soundtrack for sleep. She'd slept well the first night, immediately descending into a black cloak of stars and not stirring until they had been replaced by the first pale traces of dawn. The second night had been a sequence of naps; short interludes of oblivion before her mind became restless and required attention.

Her third night had been the strangest of the three. She'd nodded off about midnight after copious cups of camomile and the dullest pages of the most boring book she knew. But by 3am she was wide awake. Her eye mask had fallen off and she could see puffs of silvery moonlight echoing the sea just beyond the bedroom. It was too tempting not to go out. Slipping on shorts and a light sweater, she opened the door. It was July and in London it had been so hot that even the air in the parks had the fetid stench of second hand tube breath. It was cooler in Jersey, and so blissfully fresh.

The waves were still close to the sea wall, but the tide was going down. She felt blades of grass tickle her bare feet, then concrete; not that polished concrete so popular in trendy kitchens, but that rough, granular sort, where the tiny stones remind you exactly from what it is made. Stepping down onto the beach, the smell of the sea got stronger. Her feet crunched over desiccated pieces of seaweed, dry sand eventually made way for wet sand, firmer underfoot, and then, she reached the water.

Cold waves washed over ankles, over knees. It made her inhale quickly with shock. The only time she had gone in the sea at night had been on her honeymoon in the Caribbean, over a decade before. There the warm water had been like a caress on smooth tanned limbs; here it was like a harsh slap, waking up her scarred pink and white skin with a jolt. She backed away from the waves and returned up the beach. She found a set of stairs, not necessarily the ones she had come down, and climbed onto the seawall. Head tipped back into a

185

star-filled sky and eyes closed, Cassandra sat as far to the edge as she could, legs dangling over it like a doll's. Walking had been painful after the accident, but living had hurt much more.

He'd been drunk, they'd said, the police that is. He'd not have felt a thing: body so heavy, then so light, as the car took flight, her in fright. She felt it all, and still did.

"Do you feel ashamed?" the words from the boy's sister still stung. She shouldn't have gone to the funeral – that had been a mistake. Who did she think she was, intruding on their grief? The reporter must have spotted her there too and followed her back. They'd not spoken to her then, just sent a nice letter a few days later. Did she want to tell her side of events?

Did she? She wasn't sure it was her story to tell, or rather, her story that they wanted to hear. He was the "brilliant young man" the "promising medical student" the "beloved brother and smashing son." She was just the woman who took away his life; not deliberately, just by being in her car on the wrong street, at the wrong time.

The sound of the waves became softer as the tide went out. She wondered how far away it was now. She must have been there over an hour. She felt so tired; she wished she could just lie down and fall asleep. But she knew that no matter how late the time, that night, it was still too early.

His name had been. Oh, what did it matter?

She'd not been the one drinking. Maybe if she'd drunk more that night, and if he'd drunk less the roles would have been reversed. Or, more likely, nothing would have happened. She'd have called a cab. He'd have gone home from his party earlier. They'd have been in different places at different times. It would have been a different world.

Her hand had once worn a wedding ring, her body had once contained a child, her life had once had meaning. She'd come to the ocean hoping it would wash away her feelings of emptiness, her guilt and her loss. But water can only remove what is there, not what is absent. All it can give is waves and froth, tides coming in and tides going out.

They'd made her have tests, from her hospital bed, just to confirm that there wasn't anything in her blood. "Don't worry" they'd told her, when the results came back clear, "everything will be fine." But it wasn't. They'd questioned her this way and that way, and the other way some more, until she couldn't really remember what she'd been doing or why she'd been doing it. Then she was given a statement to sign, and she was dispensed, like a pharmacy prescription, sent home with a note of who she was, and what she did. The only thing she really needed was the instruction booklet telling her how to live.

It was one of those times when a list would have been handy, something specifying what to do and say when. It would have helped her get through those first few weeks when her body was on autopilot and her brain was in the passenger seat. She pushed away everyone close to her, putting up walls that needed more than a passport to get through.

People said life would eventually get back to normal, that she'd be able to forget and move on. But she couldn't. That image: eyes blank then terror-filled; skin so pale and unwrinkled, suddenly pulverised and bloody, limbs lithe and active, then cracked and motionless. She wanted to erase that

187

image but it was printed inside her head in the sort of ink you couldn't wash out. Would it fade? She hoped so much that it would.

What had the boy been thinking when he walked into the road? What thoughts went through his mind when he swayed straight into the car? If he'd felt nothing, then had he also thought nothing, or was that just a tale, constructed to make everyone feel better?

The breeze was getting up. Somewhere, far over the Atlantic, the same wind would be whipping up big waves that would slap against ships as sailors ate their chips, cause captains dismay and helmsmen to pray, of an end. She slipped off the wall back onto the sand and began walking.

Cassandra had initially tried to carry on as normal. There was food to cook, a house to clean, a job to go to, a husband to love. But gradually, each solid statement of everyday life began to fragment until her life was a suitcase of jumbled fractions. She held tight, not daring to let go in case she lost it all. No matter how broken her life was, surely she'd be able to put it together again one day? But the case was getting too heavy to carry; it was changing into a coffin.

She didn't know how to carry a coffin by herself and desperately needed somewhere to bury it. But what about the contents - the halves and quarters of her former self? If she couldn't put the fragments of her life back together, then what should she do? Could she start again, and build a new life? Only sleep would give her the clarity to make the right decisions, what to resurrect and what to leave behind.

She walked on, over damp sand, and dry, until the sky was no longer black.

And then it came to her. She didn't need sleep to help her make a decision; she needed to make a decision in order to sleep.

She'd walked further then she'd intended and sat down to rest, running fine grains of sand through her fingers. She thought about what she had lost; the unborn child, the husband, the job, the normal life. There were things she could never get back, but, enough to make it worth trying. The boy, the accident – they were not really part of her life – they were from another realm. She just had to abandon them to the sea.

She needed to sleep, so badly, she needed to sleep. The sand was soft and tempting, a mattress created for her by the relentless power of ocean against land. In the short term the land seemed immovable, but over time, the movement of the ocean would change it, erode it, and make it move.

She lay down; eyes open to a fading disco of stars. She felt warm and safe as she closed her eyes. A figure stood silently near her, watching, protecting; sprinkling her with sand until she was enveloped in a cocoon of sleep.

A message from Jersey Writers

Jersey Writers is a not-for-profit association born out of a meeting of writers at a weekend course in Jersey in 2014.

We decided to create a support and information network for writers in Jersey, the Channel Islands. This led to us establishing Jersey Writers Limited, the company that has published this anthology.

Anyone who is serious about writing can join our organisation, whether you write fiction or non-fiction, for a hobby or as a profession. We encourage all writers, from playwrights to TV and film scriptwriters, short story authors to novelists and poets to feature writers.

We are writers of all ages and all stages of our careers and the aim is to share our experiences, gain new information and advice through talks and presentations, and provide a network and single voice for what is often a lonely profession.

You are welcome to get in touch if you are a writer in Jersey. Likewise, we are keen to hear from off-island writers visiting Jersey who might like to come along and talk to us.

This is the first anthology of stories written by members of Jersey Writers. We sincerely hope you have enjoyed reading our stories. We'd love to hear from you if you have. You can contact us via the Facebook page: https://www.facebook.com/Jerseywriters or the website: www.jerseywriters.org

Printed in Great Britain
by Amazon.co.uk, Ltd.,
Marston Gate.